THE HOUSE

Visit us at www.boldstrokesbooks.com

THE HOUSE

by

Eden Darry

2019

THE HOUSE

ISBN 13: 978-1-63555-395-6

This Trade Paperback Original Is Published By
Bold Strokes Books, Inc.
P.O. Box 249
Valley Falls, NY 12185

First Edition: April 2019

CREDITS
Editor: Ruth Sternglantz
Production Design: Susan Ramundo
Cover Design By Melody Pond

PROLOGUE

I am finished. It is over. Today they arrived at the house again, and their eyes reminded me of flies, barely lighting on one place for more than a second, searching out evidence as if I would be so stupid to leave it in plain sight. They'll have to work much harder than that to catch me out. I have been here for many years.

But they *know*. They must know, and I sense that I don't have long. I've taken all the precautions I am able to, but I worry it will not be enough. They will come for me soon, and I am not ready. I could live a thousand lifetimes, and I would still not be ready. Like God moulded Lilith from clay, I moulded and shaped this house from my darkest dreams, and I am not ready to leave. I will not leave. Never.

I hear them now on the stairs and they are coming for me.

CHAPTER ONE

Fin picked up the toys scattered across the living room. She'd managed to get the kids down before eight, something she considered a bit of a feat. On the nights Sadie worked late, they were usually fussy and cranky and impossible to get to bed. Lucy was the worst. She seemed to have taken on the worst traits of her mothers, Fin's moodiness and Sadie's stubbornness, and Christ, was she stubborn. The kid would give a mule a run for its money.

Liam, on the other hand, was quiet and introspective. Unless you got his back up—then he had a temper to rival Fin's own. She grinned. She wouldn't change them for anything in the world.

Fin glanced at her watch and frowned. It was almost nine, and Sadie should be home by now. She worked as a barrister for a chambers in town and sometimes worked late when she was on a big case. Fin got a text from her this afternoon saying some new evidence had come up and she was going to be back about eight tonight.

Luckily, Fin's hours were flexible as a self-employed upholsterer, so she'd been able to knock off early and pick the kids up from the childminder. Their next door neighbour Sally looked after them during the week, and she and Sadie took it in turns to be home by six for them. Fin often ended up doing Sadie's share as well because the nature of her job meant she couldn't always leave at five.

It irked Fin a bit, even though she knew she was being unreasonable. Sadie's job paid a lot more, so it meant Fin's career took a back seat where the kids were concerned.

Fin sat on the couch which was beginning to sag in the middle—she kept meaning to sort it out—and dialled Sadie again. This time, it went straight to voicemail without ringing. She pulled one of Lucy's little plastic unicorns out from under her arse and told herself Sadie probably switched her phone off and forgot about the time. All the same, uneasiness gnawed at her. Sadie was normally good about calling when she ran late. It wasn't that they lived in a bad part of London, though stabbings and the occasional shooting weren't unheard of. These days that kind of shit was going on even in the nicest neighbourhoods—just one reason Fin kept bringing up the idea of them moving out a bit further.

Fin was born and raised on the council estate down the road, and she was sick of dirty, grimy, overcrowded London. She'd move in a heartbeat. Sadie, on the other hand, wasn't as keen. She'd grown up in London too, but much further west, where the houses didn't get much below a million pounds. While Fin was stepping over used needles and riffling down the back of the sofa for money for the electric meter key, Sadie was pissing about in ballet classes and having piano lessons. Sadie loved London—or at least, the London she knew. Fin fucking hated it.

It was well after nine now and Fin was officially worried. She tried Sadie's phone again, and again it went straight to voicemail. She hung up and dialled the chambers where Sadie worked. Voicemail again. *Shit.* As Fin was deciding whether to go next door to see if Sally could watch the kids for a couple of hours, she heard the top stair creak. Fin walked into the hall and saw Liam standing at the top looking down at her. He was still small for six, and Fin always felt particularly protective of him. There was a vulnerability about him that Lucy, stocky and noisy, didn't have.

"What's up, mate?" she asked.

"I had a bad dream," he answered, picking at the paint on the banister.

"Yeah?"

"Yeah." He nodded.

Fin walked up the stairs and lifted him into her arms. He was so light. "Let's get back into bed and you can tell me about it."

Fin lowered him into his racing car bed. She'd built the frame herself when he was three, and he refused to go into a proper sized single one yet. It was something that secretly pleased her. She pulled the covers up and tucked him in. "Okay, Liam. Tell me— what happened?"

"It was about Mummy. Something bad happened to her."

Fin's stomach lurched and she tried to keep her voice even. "Oh yeah? That sounds like a horrible dream."

Liam nodded and reached up to hold her hand. "Are you okay, Mum? Did it scare you too?"

Fin swallowed. It was hard to keep things from him. He seemed to know what you were feeling just by looking at you. "No, I'm okay, mate. What happened to Mummy in the dream?"

"A bad man got her."

Fin bit the inside of her cheek in an effort to stay calm. "It was only a dream, Liam," she whispered.

He looked up at her with his big brown eyes, and Fin was struck by how much he resembled Sadie. His brown skin was a few shades lighter than hers and his hair also brown instead of black, but they both shared those gentle, bottomless brown eyes that telegraphed every emotion they felt. Fin loved their eyes best of all.

She lifted her son's hand and gently kissed his palm. "I love you, Liam."

"I love you too." He smiled, and that was all Sadie as well.

"Go to sleep now," she whispered.

"Okay."

Fin left his door open a crack, so light from the hall would filter in, and went back downstairs. She picked up her phone to call Sally next door, but it rang in her hand before she could dial. She didn't recognize the number and her heart lurched painfully in her chest.

"Hello?" Her voice sounded steady but her hands were shaking.

"Is this Ms. Finola Claiborne?"

The voice on the other end sounded official.

"Speaking." Fin gripped the phone so hard she thought it might crack.

"I'm Detective Constable Helen Lyle, and I'm calling about your wife."

CHAPTER TWO

Fin drove faster than she probably should have, but all she could think about was getting to the hospital. At a set of red lights, she called Sadie's parents. She didn't want to, because she couldn't stand Treven Tate, Sadie's father, and the feeling was definitely mutual. He acted as though he was always in court. He even looked like a fucking judge—which was to say, down his nose at you. Fin knew he thought she was beneath his precious daughter. What Fin never let him know was, she agreed—she was punching well above her weight with Sadie.

Corine, Sadie's mother, was much nicer, and Fin got on pretty well with her. From what she'd gathered, Corine's beginnings were much the same as Fin's and she lacked the air of superiority which wafted around her husband. Corine's parents had arrived from the Caribbean after World War II, the Windrush generation, and she'd grown up poor living in a council flat on a run-down estate.

Fin already wanted to put down the phone and no one had even picked up yet. She reminded herself this wasn't about her. It was about Sadie, and she would want her father there.

DC Helen Lyle hadn't said much on the phone, except Sadie had been attacked and was conscious and alert. Just the thought of it had Fin's stomach roiling, and her hands clenched on the steering wheel involuntarily. It took effort to relax them. If someone had hurt Sadie, Fin would track the fucker down and—*and what? Kill them? Sadie and the kids would love that, wouldn't they?* Fin tried to calm herself.

She made it the hospital in record time and was met at the entrance to Accident and Emergency. "DC Lyle?"

Helen Lyle nodded and shook her hand.

"Where is she? Is she okay? What happened?" Fin fired questions and simultaneously tried to push around the policewoman and get inside the hospital.

"Ms. Claiborne, Ms. Claiborne." Helen Lyle had her hand on Fin's arm trying to restrain her.

Fin resisted the urge to push her out of the way. "I need to see my wife," she said instead.

"I know you do. She's in CT having a scan at the minute—"

"She's got a head injury?" Fin did push past her this time. She was taller than the police officer and must have outweighed her by a good fifty pounds.

"Ms. Claiborne. I need you to calm down. Right now." Helen Lyle caught up with her. "You're no good to her like this. Please. There's a family room nearby, and I can fill you in on what we know there."

Helen Lyle was right. Fin couldn't fall apart and her anger was useless. She forced herself to calm down. She blew out a breath. "Okay. Sorry."

Helen Lyle nodded and Fin followed her into a room off the main waiting area. It was painted in magnolia and had a few soft padded chairs dotted around. Fin wondered how many families had sat in here, staring at the same walls, reading the same posters about HIV and domestic abuse while waiting to hear about their loved ones.

She sat in one of the chairs and Helen Lyle in another. She steeled herself and nodded. "Go ahead."

"Your wife was attacked coming out of her chambers at about seven thirty this evening. She was dragged into an alley by her assailant. She was threatened with a knife." Helen Lyle paused and Fin could feel the other woman studying her, probably seeing if Fin would kick off again. She didn't—she wouldn't. Right now she was numb, though she knew the anger would come later.

"What did he do to her?" Her voice sounded calm, as if it came from far away. She felt like she was in a dream and she would wake up any minute.

"He took her purse and her bag. She told us he attempted to rape her but was disturbed by a group of men coming down the alley. Several of the men gave chase but he got away."

"Jesus Christ." The words came out on a breath and Fin leaned forward in her chair. She was sick and dizzy.

"Ms. Claiborne? Finola? Are you okay?"

Helen Lyle was standing over her with a hand on her shoulder, gripping lightly. The touch helped. Fin sat straighter in her chair. "I want to see my wife."

"I know. She should be back from CT shortly, and then I'll take you to her. She did suffer several blows to the head—hence the scan—and she has some nasty bruises to her face. Other than that, physically, she's fine."

"Okay." Fin felt relief at that. He hadn't stabbed her and he hadn't raped her. There was that, at least. "I called her parents. They live in Kensington so they won't be here for a bit, but—"

"I can wait for them, no problem. I'm your family liaison officer. That means I'm here to support you and Sadie and the rest of the family. I'll give you my card, so if you have any questions, you can call me any time."

"You'll tell me when you've caught the piece of shit?"

"I will. I can keep you updated on the investigation, as much as I'm able to. I'll also need you to answer a few questions when you're ready."

Fin's head came up. "Why?"

"It's nothing to worry about. Just routine stuff about your habits, whether you've noticed anyone following you. Anything unusual."

"I thought this was a mugging and attempted rape? Isn't that sort of thing random?" Fin's eyes bored into Helen Lyle's. She looked away.

"At this stage, we have to investigate every—"

"Bollocks. You think someone targeted her?"

"Ms. Claiborne, I can't give you anything at this stage. We don't know."

Fin didn't believe her, but she'd deal with that later. Right now, she wanted to see Sadie.

Helen Lyle's phone went off and she answered it. She nodded a couple of times. Fin watched her, trying to gauge what was happening.

She hung up and turned to Fin. "They've recovered the knife."

"*Knife?* You said she wasn't—"

"He used it to make her comply. He didn't use it on her. We might be able to get some useable prints."

"Okay. Okay, that's good."

"Your wife should be back by now. I'll take you to her."

Fin stood and willed herself to be calm. Sadie would need her to be solid, which meant no angry outbursts. Except Sadie always knew what she was feeling. She knew Fin's moods better than Fin did herself.

Chapter Three

Sadie closed her eyes—well, one of them anyway. The other had been closed for her by that bastard. She tried not to think about it, but she couldn't get the smell of his body odour out of her nostrils. Or the way he felt, pushed up against her, one rough hand pulling at her trousers while the other held a knife to her throat. She shivered and opened her eyes again—well, one of them.

She kept telling herself she was lucky. Lucky those men came along and scared him off. Lucky he didn't stab her right away, although she knew it was because he wanted more than just her purse. Lucky she would live to see her children and Fin again.

Fin. Sadie sighed. She hoped Fin was behaving with the police. She had a temper, and Sadie knew she was capable of lashing out when she was scared. Especially if it was to do with Sadie or the kids. She hadn't changed much from the angry twentysomething Sadie met at her twin sister Rena's party when she was nineteen.

She'd been drawn to her immediately. Back then, Fin was scruffy and looked like she needed a good meal and a bath. Sadie had thought she was a musician too, like Rena, and it was only when they started talking, Sadie realized Fin felt as out of place as her at the gathering. Sadie was in her first year of law school and about as uncool as you could get. She found out Fin was a trainee upholsterer and only there because a friend was nervous about going alone. The friend ditched Fin immediately for some hipster playing bongos in the corner.

She and Fin spent most of the evening sitting on the balcony smoking hand-rolled cigarettes and sipping from a cheap bottle of vodka Fin smuggled from the party in her worn out jean jacket. Fin told her later she was too nervous to kiss her that night, and Fin had shaken her head ruefully when Sadie confessed she'd been dying for her to. But Fin didn't bottle it the next time, and Sadie remembered it was the sweetest kiss she ever had.

She smiled at the memory despite the shooting pain in her jaw which was swollen from his punches.

She glanced up as the door opened and Fin came striding in. She looked at Sadie, her face full of horror that she quickly hid. Her short blond hair was tousled as if she'd been pulling at it and her blue eyes were glassy. Sadie reached out her hand and Fin took it gently.

"Thank God you're okay." Fin sat by the side of the bed and reached out with her other hand to smooth Sadie's hair. Sadie sighed and leaned in to the touch. "I mean, I know you're not *okay*, but—"

"I know what you mean." *Alive.* "I am okay. How are the kids?"

"Sally came over to watch them. They don't know about what happened," Fin said.

"Good. I don't want them to know."

"Babe, they're going to know something's wrong. Your face…" Fin trailed off, and Sadie saw the worry flit through her eyes.

"We'll think of something. Liam already has bad dreams. This will just make things worse."

"He had one tonight. He said a bad man…" Fin cleared her throat. "A bad man hurt you."

"Psychic Liam strikes again. He was right," Sadie said quietly.

"I'm so sorry, Sadie. I'm so sorry for what happened to you." Fin lifted Sadie's hand and Sadie smiled as Fin gently kissed her palm. "I love you."

"I love you too. We're going to be okay."

Fin nodded.

"I mean it. I won't let that bastard win."

"The police want to talk to me. About our routine and whether I've noticed anyone hanging around."

"They asked me the same thing. Have you noticed anything odd?" Sadie asked.

"No. Have you?"

"Maybe." Sadie wasn't sure how to continue. She was bound by certain rules about her clients and had to be careful what she divulged. Even to Fin.

"Sadie." Fin ducked her head and met Sadie's eyes. "Please tell me."

"I had a client a few months ago, Lance Sherry. Some things came to light which meant I couldn't represent him unless he changed his plea. He wouldn't."

"He was guilty." Fin wasn't a lawyer, but she'd been around enough of them over the years she could probably pass for one.

"I can't tell you that, Fin. He sort of threatened me—"

"*What?*"

Fin's voice took on the calm deadly tone Sadie knew well. Before Fin could explode, Sadie hurried on. "It happens, Fin. I didn't take it seriously. I thought he was just mouthing off."

"So you tell him you can't represent him, and he kicks off at you and, what, leaves?"

Sadie shifted in the bed. "No, he came to chambers one night after work. The security guard threw him out."

Fin jumped up off the bed and began to pace. "That fucking piece of shit. Who is he? What's his name again, Sadie? Why didn't you tell me?"

"Because of this, Fin. I knew you'd lose your temper. Please sit down. My head hurts and I'm tired."

Sadie watched Fin deflate as quickly as she'd exploded. She hurried back to the bed and took Sadie in her arms. "I'm sorry, babe, I'm sorry. I was so scared."

Sadie burrowed further into Fin's arms and sighed when she began to stroke her hair. This was the Fin she needed right now, the Fin who made her feel better about everything.

"I told the police about him. They're going to pick him up," Sadie said into Fin's shoulder.

"Was it him?" Fin asked, still stroking her hair.

"I'm not sure. I think so, but it was dark and I was scared. He wore a hoodie and a scarf around his face. But…I think so."

Sadie didn't tell Fin his voice sounded familiar too. If she did, Fin would want to know what he said, and she didn't think she could tell her that. It didn't stop her hearing the words in her head, though, over and over again. *Going to fuck you then kill you, bitch.* She'd told the police and that was enough.

"I called your parents. They're on their way."

"Thank you. Fin?"

"Yeah?"

"I know you won't want to, but I'd like to stay with my parents for a while. I don't want to go back to the house."

She felt Fin take a deep breath and almost smiled. "Okay. I understand."

"He took my purse. It had my keys and my driving license in it. He knows where we live." She shivered and Fin held her tighter.

"Shh, it's okay. I'll get the locks changed. You and the kids can stay at your parents until they find him."

"And you."

"Sadie…"

"I mean it, Fin. He's dangerous. I don't want you staying there either."

She felt Fin's body tense beneath her, and then she sighed.

"Okay, fine. We'll all stay with your parents. It'll be great. Your dad, especially, will be pleased to have me as a house guest," Fin said sarcastically.

Sadie elbowed her playfully and smiled. "Don't be an arsehole."

Sadie was glad her parents were coming, but all she wanted at the moment was to stay like this, with Fin hugging her and stroking her hair. For the first time all evening she felt safe.

❖

Fin went outside to call Sally and asked her to wake the kids and take them over to hers. After finding out Lance Sherry had keys to their house, she wanted them out of there. The police promised to swing by a few times over the night and check on things, which made her feel a bit better.

The doctors wanted to keep Sadie overnight for observation and were moving her up to the ward. Fin couldn't get over the sight of her, beaten black and blue. She wanted to scream and shout and hunt down the fucker who'd done it. It wouldn't help Sadie, though, and would only make things ten times worse. It was only that thought, and the way Sadie'd looked in the hospital bed—so scared and somehow small—that kept Fin from erupting.

She rubbed her eyes and breathed in the cool evening air. She felt someone watching her and turned to see a woman standing close by, smoking a cigarette. The woman smiled and held out the packet. Fin gave up smoking years ago, but right now she thought a fag was just what she needed.

"Cheers," she said.

The woman nodded and blew out a long stream of grey smoke. "You look like you need one. No offence."

Fin laughed. "None taken."

They stood side by side for a while, smoking and watching the cars go by on the main road. After a time the woman dropped her cigarette in the ashtray and went back inside.

Fin mentally ran through everything she'd need to do tomorrow. Drop the kids to school. Pack clothes and stuff for them to take to Sadie's parents. She'd take enough for a few weeks and hope they didn't have to stay longer because she might end up killing Treven if they did.

"Smoking kills."

Speak of the devil.

"Hi, Treven."

"Where's Sadie? What happened?" His deep voice was commanding, and when you combined it with his six foot two frame, she imagined he ruled his courtroom completely. The problem was, in her opinion, he ruled his family the same way.

She turned to face him and was shocked to see how scared he looked. She bit off the angry reply she had intended.

"She's okay. They're moving her up to a ward overnight. I'll take you to her."

"You should be in there with her, not smoking out here."

Fin fought the urge to snap back. Now wasn't the time. "Where's Corine?"

"Parking the car."

Typical Treven. Everyone took a back seat to his needs. "We should wait for her or she won't know where we went."

"You just want to finish your cigarette. My daughter was attacked and you're standing out here without a care in the world. What's wrong with you?"

"Fuck you, Treven," she ground out.

His eyes widened in surprise. She guessed no one ever spoke to him like that.

As if she hadn't spoken, he pointed at her and said, "I'm going inside to find out what's happening."

Just like that, she was dismissed. Fuck, she hated him. The idea of staying in his house made her want to scream.

CHAPTER FOUR

Three weeks later

Liam knew something was wrong. Ever since that horrible dream about the bad man. Neither of his parents would tell him the truth because they thought he was still a baby. He wasn't a baby— *Lucy* was a baby. He was six.

Even Lucy knew something was wrong because otherwise why would they be living with Granny and Grandad? Especially when Grandad and Mum hated each other so much. That was another thing they thought he didn't know, but he did. He wasn't stupid like they seemed to think.

Liam still remembered the dream, and he thought that somehow the bad man got out of the dream and hurt Mummy. He wasn't sure how a thing like that was possible, but it wouldn't be the first time it happened.

Once, when he was really little like Lucy, he had a dream that their neighbour Mrs. Cole got hit by a bus and squashed. The next day Mum sat him down and told him in a sad voice that Mrs. Cole had an accident and was in heaven now. It was a pity because she was a nice lady and always gave him ice pops from her freezer in the summer.

He didn't tell his mum about that dream because he was worried it might be his fault for dreaming about it. Maybe the bus drove right out of his dream and squashed Mrs. Cole from next door?

Liam didn't know anyone else who had dreams like that, and he was fairly certain neither of his parents did. He wondered about the bad man from his dream and why he would want to hurt Mummy. He also wondered how he got out of the dream, and if there was any way to keep him in next time. Liam hoped there was, because he had another one last night.

In that dream the bad man came back.

❖

Sadie could hear Fin and her dad in the other room. This week, they were being coldly polite to each other. Sadie wasn't sure which she preferred—this, or them bickering. They were driving her crazy.

They'd never got on from the start. The first time Sadie brought Fin home, her father looked her up and down like he was observing something in a Petri dish. Despite what he often said to Sadie, Fin wasn't stupid and cottoned on quickly that Treven Tate thought she wasn't good enough for his daughter.

The most frustrating thing—something she could never tell either of them—was her dad and Fin were so much alike. And though they would deny it strenuously, they really did have a lot in common. Like Fin, Treven came from a rough council estate and was raised by a single mother. Unlike Fin's mum, though, Sadie's grandmother spent every penny she had making sure her dad got a good education.

Even so, Fin hadn't done badly either. She'd told Sadie it had been touch and go for a while, when she got in with the wrong crowd and left school without doing any exams. But she sorted herself out and became an upholsterer. Last year, she started her own business. Fin liked to play it down, but Sadie knew she was good. Really good. She was starting to get clients from overseas through recommendations, and Sadie knew it wouldn't be long before the business was extremely successful.

Sadie wished Fin didn't feel so inferior all the time. She knew her father didn't help, always insinuating things and making veiled insults about her intelligence. Although, to be fair, it wasn't all his doing. Fin liked to needle him whenever possible. Somehow, they always managed to bring out the worst in each other.

For the first week they stayed with her parents, her dad and Fin were on best behaviour. It helped that Fin was out of the house at six, driving across town to drop Liam at school, then going to work, and back at eight after collecting them from Sally. She was too tired to fight with Sadie's dad.

But when it became clear Lance Sherry had gone to ground and wouldn't be found as easily as they first thought, they'd hired a childminder closer to Kensington, and Sadie's mum picked Liam up from school for them. So Fin was around more, and the fighting had escalated.

Sadie hadn't said anything to Fin yet, but she didn't think she could ever go back to their house.

She knew Fin changed the locks and Lance Sherry wouldn't be stupid enough to hang around the house, but all the same, when she thought about going home, her chest got tight and she found it hard to breathe.

The counsellor she was seeing told her this was normal. Panic attacks were common and nothing to be ashamed of. But she could barely manage a trip to the local shop without one of these panic attacks coming on. If someone got too close, or came up behind her on the pavement, she freaked out and she hated herself for it.

She knew it was normal, she'd been through a trauma, blah, blah, blah. Sadie just wanted her life back. She wanted to be able to take the kids to the park without crying when a jogger ran past her. She wanted to go out to dinner with Fin and not freak out if the restaurant lighting was too dim and she couldn't see other patrons' faces clearly, terrified Lance Sherry would be seated at one of the tables.

She was sick and tired of constantly wondering where he was and whether he was coming for her to make good on his promise to fuck her and kill her.

In the next room, something crashed to the floor and she screamed.

❖

"Are you sure you're okay?" Fin hovered by the door and Sadie wanted to yell at her to go away.

"I'm fine. For the millionth time, Fin," she snapped and immediately felt horrible. Fin was just trying to help. She'd been next door with Sadie's dad trying to put together a plastic playhouse for Lucy's birthday when it fell apart on them. In a way, it was almost good she'd screamed and had a panic attack because it stopped the inevitable shouting match that would have ensued. "I'm sorry. I didn't mean to snap at you." She patted the bed beside her.

Fin hesitated, then came in and stretched out alongside her. Sadie snuggled into her. "Fin, we have to get out of this house. Before I kill either you or my dad."

Fin laughed. "Believe it or not, we're both trying to be nice to each other. He only called me thick twice today, and I only thought about murdering him once."

Sadie slapped her belly playfully. "We need to get out of here," she repeated.

"No argument from me. I outstayed my welcome back in 2002. You want to move back to the house?"

Sadie fought down the panic which bloomed in her chest at the thought of going home. "No. I can't go back there, Fin. Ever. Even when he's caught, he'll still know our address, and he could tell other people. He's a nasty piece of work, and I'd always be worried who was knocking on the door. Do you think I'm being silly?"

"Of course I don't think you're being silly. Besides, you've got a lot to deal with at the moment. Whatever you want, we'll do, okay?"

"I knew there was a reason I married you," she joked.

"We know it wasn't for my brains," Fin said.

"Don't do that, Fin. You aren't stupid. I love my dad, but he's a terrible snob. Don't let him make you feel bad."

Fin was silent and Sadie waited, betting she would change the subject. Fin rarely talked about the emotional stuff, especially where it concerned her vulnerabilities.

"I can put the house on the market tomorrow," Fin said.

"Thank you. My dad offered to help us if we wanted to buy further out this way."

She felt Fin stiffen. "Do you want to live around here?" Fin asked quietly. Under ordinary circumstances, Fin would have gotten angry at the suggestion, and Sadie loved her for trying so hard not to blow up.

"No. I told him we don't need any money," Sadie said. "I knew you wouldn't want it."

"He would throw it back in my face every chance he got."

Sadie didn't say anything because it was true. "I've been thinking about where we'd move to."

"You want to leave the area, then?"

"Yes. I think so. Do you still want to move out of London?" Fin shifted beneath her and looked down with hope in her eyes. Sadie smiled. "I was thinking we could try the outskirts, maybe? That way, when I go back to work, it won't be a long commute. Or I could get a job closer to where we live. You'd be able to work from home if we got somewhere with an outbuilding. Though I'm not sure we'd have the budget for that." Sadie was aware she was rambling. The truth was, she wasn't sure if this was what *she* wanted at all. She was feeling scared and vulnerable, and suddenly the idea of Fin's country dream started to appeal to her in a way it hadn't before.

If they stayed fairly near to town, it wouldn't be too much of a change. She was trying to convince herself, she knew.

"Are you sure, babe? I mean, you weren't interested before. It might be just a reaction to what's happened."

Sometimes, Fin was clueless about how Sadie was feeling. Other times, like now, she could read her perfectly.

"It is, partly. But there's another part of me that thinks it's a good idea. It would be great for the kids, and we wouldn't be so far from London that I couldn't go in whenever I wanted."

"And work? It's a longer commute, maybe a few hours. We couldn't get anywhere with land in a reasonable distance to town."

Sadie didn't want to think about work right now. She'd been signed off and was thinking of handing in her notice, though she hadn't told Fin yet. She wasn't sure if she could go back when she'd been attacked right outside her chambers. Her dad would have something to say about it as well. A lot of things to say about it. She didn't care, though. She'd spent her life doing what pleased him—university, law degree, and then becoming a barrister. He had hopes of her becoming a judge like him, she knew.

Since the attack, she'd felt something inside her shift. She understood how fragile her life was because for a few moments, someone else held it in his hands. Sadie was living her father's life and maybe she didn't want to any more. Maybe she wanted some time to figure out what sort of life she *did* want. Maybe fresh air and country living would help her do that.

"Put the house on the market, Fin. Start looking at places out of London. Just, not *too* country, though. Okay?"

Fin laughed and squeezed her. "Okay. Not *too* country. I'll get on it tomorrow."

CHAPTER FIVE

Fin chose a table near the back of the pub, away from the band tuning their instruments and the rowdy kids playing pool. *Kids.* She was definitely getting old to be calling people kids, Jesus.

She sipped her lager and grinned when Rose pushed her way through the crowd and started waving like an idiot when she saw Fin. This week, her hair was pink and she wore her multicoloured tights and purple Doc Martens.

Fin met her at school. They hadn't exactly been friends, but both found themselves outside the head's office together on a few occasions, Fin for skipping school or mouthing off to a teacher, and Rose for getting another piercing or refusing to wash out the brightly coloured dye from her hair. They lost touch after Fin dropped out and met again in Lips, a women's bar in town, one night when they were eighteen.

One thing led to another, and Rose ended up taking Fin home. The sex was pretty decent, and they'd done it again a few times before deciding they were much better off as friends. Now, Fin considered Rose her very best friend. She'd stuck by Fin even at her most twattish and was godmother to both kids.

"Love the hair." Fin stood and kissed Rose on the cheek.

"Thank you." Rose gave a little curtsy before sitting down and pulling a pint towards her. She had the tiniest hands and Fin was always reminded of a toddler when Rose held a pint glass. "How's Sadie?"

"She's okay, thanks. A bit better. She wants to sell the house."

"I don't blame her. That prick knows where it is. How are you? And don't give me your usual bullshit. How are you *really*?"

How was she? Rose was the only one who ever asked. Everybody wanted to know about Sadie, and of course that was right and normal. She'd been through hell and Fin felt selfish when the little voice inside whined, *But what about me?* True, she hadn't been through the attack and couldn't even imagine how terrible it must have been—she still had to batten down the rage when she thought about it. But she was also the one who shook Sadie awake at night when she was having a nightmare and held her while she sobbed. She was the one who had to make up a story to the kids about why they were living with Granny and Grandad and why Mummy's face was black and blue. And make up more stories about why she wasn't herself lately.

So sometimes, yeah, she did want to be asked how she was doing, because the attack hadn't left her untouched either. "I think if I have to live with Treven for another week, I'm going to blow my brains out. Or his. I'm not sure."

Rose brayed with laughter. A few people turned around to stare at them. She had a horrendous laugh which also, somehow, made you want to laugh along with her. "I only met him once, and I can see why you'd want to kill him. He's number six my top ten list of bastards."

"I thought whatshisname, that plumber you were shagging, was number six."

"I've bumped him down. It's been four years, Fin. Holding on to negative shit isn't good for you," she said sagely. Rose went on a self-awareness course she got half price through Groupon the previous month.

"Says the woman with the top ten list of bastards." Fin smiled and shook her head. "How are you, anyway? I see you've dyed your hair."

"I'm great. It's called Passion Pink. And it's making quite a difference to my love life already."

"Do tell."

"I finally managed to bag the dog walker woman."

Fin clapped enthusiastically. "Well played. Does this mean you can stop pretending to be a jogger now?"

"Yes, thank God. Getting up at six every Wednesday was killing me."

"Have you slept with her yet?" Fin asked.

Rose eyed her sceptically. "Don't think I don't know what you're doing."

"What do you mean?"

"You haven't answered my question. I asked how you were." Rose leaned forward and raised her eyebrows.

Fin shifted and looked away. "I told you already. I hate living with Treven."

"Fin, you're starting to piss me off."

"Okay, fine. Fine." Fin held up her hands in surrender. "I'm okay. Some days I still want to find the fucker who hurt her and rip his head off—every day, really. It's hard to lie to the kids as well. Especially Liam—Lucy's still too young to really question me."

"Liam's smart. He sees a lot."

"I know. I catch him watching sometimes, trying to work out what we aren't telling him. I hate lying, but Sadie doesn't want him to know. He already has nightmares. On a happier note, Sadie wants me to sell the house."

"Why's that a happy note?" Rose downed the last of her pint. Fin was still only halfway through hers.

"She wants to do the country move. Told me to start looking for somewhere."

Rose narrowed her eyes. "Is she doing this because of what happened? I mean, what if she wakes up in a year and realizes the move was a massive mistake?"

Fin shrugged. "Then I guess we move back. I did ask her if she was sure."

"And? What did she say?"

"She wants to move to the country. What am I supposed to do? Refuse?"

"Maybe wait a while? It's only been three weeks since she was, you know, attacked. Why don't you hang on a bit longer?"

"I can't stay there, Rose. I'm serious, I can't stand Treven. I think he hates me, and I know I hate him. It isn't good for the kids or Sadie. The atmosphere is terrible. If Sadie didn't need me, I'd have moved back to the house until it sold."

"Yeah, okay, I get that. You can always stay with me—all of you."

"You live in a studio flat, Rose."

Rose looked indignant. "It has a mezzanine level."

"How would the dog walker feel about you sharing your flat with a family of four?"

"We stay at her place. It's nicer."

"Thanks, mate, I do appreciate the offer but I think I'll just find us somewhere to rent until the house sells and we buy somewhere else."

Rose nodded. "Offer's always open."

"Thanks. So, tell me more about the dog walker."

Rose laughed. "Let's get another drink and I'll fill you in."

Sadie held out her glass and Rachel poured her some more wine. They were sitting in her parents' conservatory. She and Rachel Moses met at university and dated for a couple of months. Like Fin, Rachel was tall and pale with short blond hair. The similarity ended there, though. Rachel was ice with a sharp tongue that could cut you off at the knees. Sadie had been on the end of it a few times when they were lovers. The relationship hadn't worked out, but the friendship had, and Sadie was grateful for it now because, apart from Fin, Rachel was the most loyal person she knew.

"Are you absolutely sure about this move?" Rachel asked for the third time. Sometimes, she could be like Sadie's father, asking the same question until she got the answer she wanted.

"Yes, Rachel. I won't go back to the house, and Fin always wanted to move out of London—"

"Which is fine for her. She can sew up sofas wherever, I imagine." Rachel waved her hand dismissively. "You're a barrister, for God's sake."

"I can do that in places other than London as well," Sadie replied, ignoring the jibe at Fin.

"It's not the same and you know it."

"Don't be a snob, Rachel." Sadie sipped her wine and noted it was her favourite. Rachel always bought her favourite.

"I'm not. Well, okay, maybe I am. I'm selfish and I want you to stay here."

Sadie laughed. "I'm not going to the moon. We'll be an hour at most outside of London."

"In the country." Rachel raised one eyebrow.

"It's not even the country, Rachel. It has the Central Line. It's a twenty-minute drive from North London."

Rachel pursed her lips. "It's not the same."

Sadie sighed. How could she explain this to her? "After Lance Sherry attacked me, when I realized I might never see my kids or Fin again, I did a lot of thinking. I work ridiculous hours, and I hardly get to see them as it is. At weekends, I'm sitting at the kitchen table with a pile of paperwork, and they're off to the zoo or the park. I get home after they've gone to bed most nights. For the first time, I don't have anything to do except think. I don't know if I want to be a barrister any more. It was always my dad's dream, anyway, not mine."

"You didn't want to be a barrister?" Rachel asked, looking at Sadie like she'd grown a second head.

"I don't know what I wanted to be. I didn't get the chance to find out."

"So you're going to bum around the countryside contemplating your navel? What will you live on?" Rachel asked sceptically.

Sadie knew the conversation would go like this. She was using it as a practice run for her father.

"You don't need to worry about that, Rachel. You won't be the one having to support me."

"No, Fin will. On a pittance," she shot back.

"That's enough." Sadie was sick of people running Fin down. "She doesn't earn a pittance, and even if she did, it's got bloody nothing to do with you."

"I'm sorry, I'm sorry." Rachel leaned forward and put her hand on Sadie's knee. "That was out of order. I shouldn't have said it."

"No, you shouldn't."

"I'm worried about you, Sadie. You were horribly attacked, and now you're telling me you're jacking in your job and moving to the countryside. It's a lot to take in."

Sadie sighed. It was a lot to take in. She hadn't even told Fin about her job yet. She hadn't really thought about money either. They had some savings, and Fin did earn enough to tide them over for a while, contrary to what her father and Rachel thought. After that, though? What would they do? What would *she* do? She still didn't know.

"Whatever you decide, Sadie, I'm here for you. Despite the fact I can be a selfish arsehole, I do love you."

Sadie smiled. "I know. And you aren't an arsehole. Often."

Rachel grinned. "Thanks. If you need money—"

"Thank you, but no."

"But I—"

"No, Rachel. We're fine. We can manage."

Rachel nodded, though she looked like she wanted to say more. Sadie wouldn't take money from her, or her father. For the first time, she and Fin would be doing what they wanted to do, what was best for their family, and they didn't need anybody else's help.

CHAPTER SIX

One month later

Fin checked the price on the property details again. The estate agent had emailed them over that morning and Fin couldn't believe the house was in their price range. She'd called their office to make sure it wasn't a misprint and booked an appointment that afternoon to view it.

There must be something wrong with it, she thought, while she waited at the end of the lane as the agent had instructed her. Fin judged the house to be about ten minutes from the tube station by car. It had five bedrooms, backed onto farmland, and had its own outbuilding complete with electricity and running water. The previous owners were in the middle of renovating it when they'd had to return to France in a hurry because of a family emergency. It seemed unlikely they would be able to come back, so they'd put the house on the market and priced it low for a quick sale.

Even so, it was well below market value for this area, and Fin couldn't understand why. They could have put it on for fifty thousand more, and it still would have been cheap. Life had taught her you didn't get anything for nothing and there was always a catch. She'd probably get inside and see there was subsidence or a horrendous damp problem. It didn't look that way in the photos, but pictures could be touched up.

The agent arrived bang on twelve thirty and pulled up alongside her car. She rolled down the window. "Fin?"

"Yeah. Gemma?"

"That's me. Hop in and I'll drive us up there. It's tricky to find. Your car will be fine there."

Fin got in the car and Gemma started up the lane at a snail's pace. She glanced sheepishly over at Fin. "I've been here twice and still miss the turn every time."

Fin smiled. "Look, I don't mean to be rude, but what's wrong with this place?"

For a moment, Gemma looked alarmed, then glanced over at Fin with her estate agent's smile firmly in place. "Everyone asks that. It's a great house, I promise. The owners hadn't gotten around to completely modernizing it, but it's structurally sound. They really need a quick sale."

"Because of a family emergency."

Gemma's smile faltered again. "Right."

"Right." Fin sighed and turned to look out the window. Gemma wasn't going to give her any more than that. Besides, she'd see what the problem was for herself in a minute.

Gemma didn't miss the turn this time, and before long they were parked outside a beautiful Victorian house. The front garden was overgrown, and litter and weeds covered the gravel drive, but none of that detracted from the house.

"It still retains most of the original features—the stained glass around the door, and another gorgeous stained glass window as you go up the stairs."

Fin followed Gemma inside the house, and it was just as lovely as the outside. Patterned tiles lined the hallway—again, original—and the architraves, plaster ceiling roses, and cornices all remained. As they walked around the ground floor, Fin saw the previous owners had finished most of the work down here. There was a large kitchen with a working fire and two big reception rooms and a utility room. A conservatory at the back opened onto the garden, which was a complete wilderness at the moment. Fin couldn't help imagining them all out here in the summer, a barbecue on the go and a tree house for the kids to mess about in. She smiled.

Upstairs was a little shabbier. It still had the original features, but the hall carpet was mouldy and lining paper was peeling off the walls. There were a lot of water stains on the ceiling.

"Looks like the roof's knackered." Fin pointed to a particularly big stain in the front bedroom.

"It may need some attention," Gemma conceded.

The bathrooms were pretty awful seventies jobs and would need to be replaced at some point, but they seemed fairly functional for now. Why anyone had ever thought an avocado coloured suite was trendy was beyond Fin.

It was the loft bedroom which did it for Fin. The owners hadn't spared much expense up here. There were new carpets and a walk-in cupboard—a dressing room according to Gemma—and the attached bathroom had a roll-top bath and something Gemma called a rain-forest shower. As far as Fin could see, it just meant there were two showerheads instead of one. Sadie would probably like it, though.

"What do you think?"

They were back in the kitchen, and Fin was desperately trying not to show how much she wanted the house. "I have a few concerns, but it looks good."

Gemma smiled as if she knew Fin was full of shit. "We've already had a lot of interest, so I don't think it's going to be around for long."

"Right," Fin replied. She looked up at the wall and frowned. *That's weird.* "There is one thing. I've noticed some slightly odd features. The house is structurally sound, isn't it?"

"I believe so. What sort of things?" Gemma asked.

"In some of the rooms, there's vents on the internal walls. Or that door in the second bedroom that doesn't have an internal handle."

"Well, it's an old house, you know. Lots of quirks, bits fall off. It's probably been remodelled over the years—it was built in 1886, you know."

"I suppose," Fin agreed. But why would you have a door opening onto a wall? Unless it led somewhere originally. Maybe she'd get hold of the original blueprints and see what work had been done. If they got the house, that was. Sadie still needed to see it. "I'd like to bring my wife for a look if that's okay?"

"Of course. Let's go back to the car and book in a time."

Fin followed Gemma outside. She took one last look at the house and knew she wanted it. Even though it needed further renovation, there was something about it that spoke to her. She felt like she'd come home.

❖

"Is this normal?" Sadie whispered, standing beside Fin as they stood waiting in the lane near the house.

"What? Waiting here or viewing it with another couple?" Fin whispered back.

"Well, both."

Fin grinned. "Apparently it's hard to find, and about the other"—she nodded over at the couple standing by their brand new BMW—"I don't know."

The truth was, as soon as Fin saw them—Grant and Bev—her heart sank. It was true you couldn't always judge a book by its cover, but they looked minted—rich. They could probably outbid her and Sadie all day long. What made it worse was she didn't like them. Grant's beady little eyes kept raking over Sadie, and Bev was looking at them as if they were aliens. Fin doubted she'd ever seen real-life lesbians before. Grant, on the other hand, was probably imagining all the lesbian porn he'd ever watched, with Sadie in the starring role.

Fin was relieved when Gemma pulled up. "Hi, everyone. Fin, did you and Sadie want to follow me up in your car? Grant and Beth can come with me." She favoured them with what was probably her best smile.

Fin nodded. So Gemma thought Grant and Bev were the most likely couple to get the house too. She sighed.

Fin studied Sadie's face as they walked round the house, trying to guess what she was thinking. It felt a bit like introducing your new girlfriend to your best friend and praying they would like each other. Gemma pretty much left them to their own devices, telling them Fin had been here before so just to look around and let her know if they had any questions.

"Well? What do you think?" Fin couldn't contain herself any longer. They had been all the way around, and she couldn't tell what Sadie was thinking.

"You really love it, don't you?" Sadie smiled.

"Is it that obvious?"

"Yes, darling. You're like Lucy with a new unicorn toy."

"Christ, I'm not that manic, am I?"

Sadie laughed. "Almost."

"What do you think, though? Do you like it?"

"Umm…yes."

"You don't sound sure. You're doing that thing where you furrow your brow."

"I do like it. I mean, it needs work upstairs, but it's a good size. The location is excellent, and the price is so low for what it is."

"But?"

"I'm not sure. I don't know. Maybe I'm still getting used to the idea of moving out of London."

Fin studied her. Sadie did seem much better this last week. She'd been out to the shops alone a few times, and the panic attacks weren't coming as frequently. She wasn't all the way back to her old self. Sometimes Fin wondered if she ever would be.

She'd changed since the attack, which was probably normal, and in some ways it was positive change. She'd told Fin she wasn't sure about being a barrister any more, that it had always been her father's dream and she'd just gone along with it.

"Babe, if you don't want to move out of London, we don't have to. It's okay if you've changed your mind." Fin stroked Sadie's shoulder down to her arm and took her hand. "Just say the word, and we'll look for something in town. Okay?"

Sadie put her arms around her neck and pulled her in for a kiss. "I love you, Fin Claiborne. We should offer on the house."

"Really?" Fin drew her in and squeezed. "Are you sure?"

"Yes, I'm sure."

Fin thought she sounded more confident this time. "Thank you, Sadie. Thank you."

Someone cleared their throat behind them and they turned, still in each other's arms. Sadie broke away when she saw Bev's hand.

"Oh my God, what happened?" she asked.

Fin looked down and saw Bev's hand was bleeding quite badly.

"Fucking nail sticking out of the wall," Grant ground out. His face was red and Fin could practically see him tossing up in his mind whether to try and sue.

"You should go to hospital," Sadie said, unwinding the scarf from her neck. "Here, wrap this around it."

When no one made a move to take it from her, she wrapped it around Bev's hand herself and pulled it tight.

"Thanks," Bev said weakly.

"Come on, let's get out of this deathtrap," Grant said and took his wife by the arm.

Gemma gave Fin a watery smile. "That was unfortunate."

Fin bet she could see her commission floating out of reach.

"Yeah. I know you had high hopes for them. We want to make an offer. Asking price," Fin said more confidently than she felt.

There would be more Grant and Bevs with more money than her and Sadie. She knew the chances were high they would be outbid. But she wanted the house. A lot.

Gemma nodded. "Okay. I'll drive them back to their car and let the owners know."

She hurried out of the house, leaving Sadie and Fin alone.

"Poor Bev," Sadie said and shook her head.

"Yeah, poor Bev," Fin echoed, when what she was really thinking about was whether the nail would be enough to put them off buying the house. Somehow, she doubted it.

Fin was in her workshop picking at a salad when her phone rang. She'd decided to break for lunch and was considering packing work in and going home. Fin was so preoccupied with thoughts of the house, she'd barely got anything done and the work was starting to pile up. The only thing stopping her from knocking off early was the thought of spending more time with Treven.

Her heart thumped in her chest when she saw it was Gemma, the estate agent, calling.

"Hi, Gemma," she answered.

"Ms. Claiborne. How are you?"

"I'm good. Is there news on our offer?" Fin asked, not holding out much hope.

"Yes, I'm pleased to say it's been accepted."

Fin's heart triple timed, and she barely resisted the urge to let out a whoop. "That's great news. I honestly thought we would be outbid by Grant and Bev," she said and managed to keep the excitement out of her voice.

Gemma was silent on the other end and Fin thought they'd been cut off. In a quieter voice, she said, "Bev died."

Fin thought she'd misheard. "What? Did you say *died?*"

"Yes. She got septicaemia and then it turned into sepsis."

"That's awful." Fin wanted the house, but she didn't want it at the expense of Bev's life. "Was it from that nail?"

"That's what her husband says. He wants to sue. Look, I shouldn't really be talking about this." Gemma sounded nervous.

"No, of course not. I don't want to put you in an awkward position."

"Thanks. I just thought you should know." She hesitated. "Do you still want the house?"

Why wouldn't she? "Yes, definitely. Just do me a favour and don't mention this to Sadie. She's had a rough few months, and I don't want to make things worse."

"Okay."

They spoke for a few more minutes, exchanging solicitors' details and other information. When Fin hung up, the news about Bev had dampened her enthusiasm slightly, though she was still over the moon about the house. She felt less good about keeping Bev's death a secret from Sadie. Fin told herself Sadie had enough to deal with at the moment, but a quiet voice in the back of her head wondered if it was more to do with being afraid of Sadie deciding against the house if she knew.

Fin decided not to think about it any more. What was done was done, and they needed to move forward. The house was going to be a fresh start for all of them. Bev's death was tragic, but it certainly had nothing to do with the house.

CHAPTER SEVEN

Four months later

Sadie folded one of Lucy's T-shirts and put it in the suitcase before zipping it closed. The house sale and purchase of the new one had gone smoothly, and today they were moving in.

Fin was with the removal guys at the old house, packing up the last of the furniture, and would meet Sadie and the kids at the new place. She still hadn't been back to the house. The panic attacks came less often now, but she still couldn't bring herself to go back there, and even thinking about it made her chest tight. It didn't help that the police still hadn't found Lance Sherry—she'd assumed that with all the CCTV and other technology around, it would have been quick and easy.

Their family liaison officer, Helen, told her and Fin they thought he'd managed to go abroad. From what Sadie gathered, Sherry was well connected in the criminal world, and it wouldn't have been too much trouble for him to get out of the UK. It would take years to track him down and potentially even longer to have him extradited if he'd gone outside the EU.

She sighed and sat on the bed. Fin and the kids were so excited about moving, and all she felt was a peculiar sort of dread. She didn't understand it. True, she hadn't fallen in love with the house like Fin, but she didn't hate it either. When she tried to think about what was bothering her, she was overcome with tiredness and her thoughts became muddled.

It was probably her poor overworked brain's way of putting a stop to all the worrying. Sadie had always been a planner and a thinker, while Fin was happier to go where the wind took her. Before, Sadie had enjoyed the way her mind worked, but since the attack it was like she'd overloaded it. Her thoughts had always been crisp and clear and logical, but now she felt like she was slogging through thick fog. She felt dull, and all the edges now rippled and wavered.

The psychologist she was seeing helped. She made Sadie feel like she was normal, that her reactions and responses were okay. Maybe they were, for now. Maybe all she needed was time to adjust and rest. This move would do that for her. She hadn't even thought about her job, and the chambers were being incredibly understanding. They'd given her three months' wages with her severance, which was generous. Combined with Fin's pay, they would be fine for a while yet. Maybe she'd take up knitting and join the Women's Institute. Sadie was struck by an image of herself as a fifties housewife and laughed.

"Care to share the joke?"

Sadie turned at the voice of her father in the doorway. He was a big man with wide shoulders. Sadie had a memory of him carrying her on those shoulders, his large hands holding on to her little girl legs, warm and strong. His hair was more grey than black now, but he still looked much younger than sixty-three. Sadie knew she favoured him more in looks and height, although she had her mother's slender frame.

"I was thinking about joining the Women's Institute," she joked.

Her father smiled. "Your grandmother would be proud. Have you finished packing?"

She watched him hover in the doorway and could tell he had something to say.

"Dad. You didn't come up here to help me with packing." She patted the bed beside her and he came and sat.

"I know it sounds silly, but I don't want you to go."

"Oh, Dad." She leaned in to him.

"I know, I know." He stood again before she could put an arm around him. Treven Tate wasn't comfortable with displays of physical affection—except when she and Rena were little. She remembered him cuddling them all the time back then.

"You were like this the last time I moved out."

He grinned. "I told you, I wasn't crying when you left for university. It was my allergies."

"It was September, Dad."

They both laughed, then looked at each other. She'd always been the apple of her father's eye. Unfortunately for Rena, he'd never hidden it very well. "After what happened...I feel like I don't want you to leave. You're safe here with me."

Sadie was surprised he'd voiced his feelings—he so rarely did. "I'll be safe there too. Fin had an alarm system installed yesterday."

"Did she?" He looked surprised.

"Yes, Dad. I know you think she's stupid, that she isn't good enough for me"—Sadie held up her hand when he tried to interrupt—"but she's smart and she cares and she wants me to be safe, just like you do."

He sighed and sat beside her again. This time his arm came around her shoulders, and he pulled her close. "Truthfully, I don't think anyone would be good enough for you. Fin isn't so bad. She's just...rough around the edges."

"She's a great mother and a loving wife. She treats me well, and you should be happy about that."

"I am."

"But?"

"I'll try harder with her. Okay?"

"You always say that."

"This time I mean it. We could have lost you, and I—" He cleared his throat. "Your mother has given me some…points for consideration relating to my behaviour."

Sadie rolled her eyes. "You mean she had a go at you about the way you treat Fin."

He grinned sheepishly. "Something like that."

"It would be nice if the two of you could be civil at least. Especially for Liam and Lucy. They see what goes on."

"I know. I'll try, okay, sweetheart?" He kissed the top of her head and gave her one last squeeze before standing up. "Shall I bring down the case?"

"Thanks, Dad."

Sadie opened the other suitcase on the bed and continued packing.

❖

Lance Sherry stepped off the ferry and breathed deeply. *Home.* He adjusted the bag on his shoulders and made his way into the terminal, where he'd booked a seat on a bus back to London. When he first ducked out and went abroad, it was with the intention to stay gone, but he couldn't get her out of his head. The way she'd dismissed him as unworthy of her time. It grated on him, and if he was honest, Lance Sherry wasn't used to being told no. Not by a woman, anyway.

He probably hadn't been away long enough for the heat to die down, and he was taking a big risk. If he was lucky, he could get in and get back out again before anyone noticed. Except he wasn't lucky last time. All he could hope for was that he would be able to at least give the bitch what she had coming to her before the police caught up with him.

Lance Sherry climbed onto the bus and took a seat near the back. He scratched his face, which itched where the beard now grew. He couldn't wait to shave the bloody thing off.

CHAPTER EIGHT

Fin stood in the workshop and couldn't help but smile. The skylights would flood the room with light once she'd cleaned them up, and the large open space was perfect for her work. There was a stack of boxes in the corner she would have to shift, but that shouldn't be hard. The basement would be more difficult because previous owners had stored decades' worth of junk down there. Boxes and bits of broken furniture littered the place. Fortunately, it was dry, so she wouldn't be shifting soggy boxes and mouldy furniture. The estate agent gave her the number of a local lad who did odd jobs and would be happy to help. Floyd Dodson. He'd done odd jobs around the place for the previous owners, and his mother was the local childminder.

The house was perfect for them. It was true Sadie hadn't fallen in love with it like her, but there was time. It was the sort of place Fin dreamed of living as a kid. The garden was huge, with fields spread out behind. They could get a dog if Sadie was up for it. Fin always wanted a dog. She'd ordered one of those playsets for the kids as a surprise as well. Lucy would love it.

For the first time, Fin felt a sense of achievement. She'd made this happen for her family. Finola Claiborne—with the pisshead mother and thieving father who did a moonlight flit when she was ten—now had a beautiful barrister wife, two great kids, and her own business. No one would have guessed that for her. And from today, she had the house to go with it all.

Outside, a car crunched up the gravel drive and stopped in front of the house. Car doors opened and she heard the voices of her children. Lucy was the loudest by far. Fin grinned.

"We drove past the turn off twice. Hidden away, isn't it?" Sadie called through the open window.

"I didn't have any trouble finding it," she said, walking out into the sunshine.

"Mama!" Lucy yelled and charged at her. Fin braced herself for the impact of the three-year-old and swung her up into her arms.

"You like the place, Lucy-loo?" she asked, looking into brown eyes and brushing at a tangle of thick brown curls, almost golden in the sunlight.

"Yes! Can we go inside?"

Liam hadn't spoken properly until he was almost four, but Lucy was a regular chatterbox. Fin loved that you could have proper conversations with her already—well, as long as the conversations were about unicorns or bugs. She loved hunting for bugs.

"Liam, you want to go inside?" Fin asked her son.

His brow was creased in the way Sadie's did when she wasn't sure about something. "Okay," he replied quietly. Fin followed his gaze up to the first floor, as the frown on his little forehead deepened.

"Then you can help me bring in the stuff from the car," Sadie said, walking over to kiss Fin on the lips and ruffle Lucy's hair. "Lucy, how did your hair get so tangled?" she asked.

"She opens the window all the way in the car and tries to stick her head out like a dog," Liam supplied.

"Me not a dog," Lucy said, letting go of Fin and folding her arms across her chest.

"*I'm* not a dog," Sadie said, ruffling her hair again.

"Me and Mummy not dogs," she corrected herself.

Fin and Liam burst into laughter.

"Hilarious," Sadie deadpanned. "Go inside, all of you. Liam gets first pick of the bedrooms, Lucy, okay?"

"Okay." Lucy wriggled out of Fin's arms and ran for the front door. She never seemed to walk anywhere.

❖

Liam looked around his new bedroom. It was bigger than his old room but he didn't like it any better. He liked their old house, and he didn't understand why they had to move away. He didn't want a new start, even though his mum said it would be good for them.

Liam liked his old school and his old friends and his old house. He didn't like this house at all. When Mummy stopped the car, he thought he saw a man in the upstairs window. When he got out, the man was gone, and he guessed he'd just imagined it after all. They'd driven past the house two times before Mummy found the entrance. It was like it didn't want them to find it. Now that he was inside, he got a feeling the house didn't want them here—especially Mummy. Perhaps the man had been real after all. Maybe he lived here and he didn't like children.

Down the hall, a door slammed, and Liam jumped.

❖

Lance Sherry had been watching the house most of the day. No one had come in or gone out. Just his luck, they'd be on holiday. It didn't matter—he'd wait as long as he needed for the bitch to come home.

It was afternoon already, and he wanted to get inside before people started coming back from work. Apart from some workmen a few houses down, the street was quiet, and he didn't think he'd have any trouble breaking in unnoticed.

He crossed the road leisurely and slipped into the passage that ran down between the houses and then along the back of their gardens. Places like these were always the easiest to rob, and he was constantly amazed residents didn't club together to get gates for the passage entrances. They'd remained in place from the days when people still got coal delivered. The coalman would come down the passage and tip the coal directly into bins or whatever at the bottom of people's gardens. It was so easy to slip in and out without being noticed.

Lance turned right at the end of the passage and pushed on the garden gate. It held, but it was flimsy. He put his shoulder into it and popped the bolt out from the other side. Piece of piss.

He was careful to listen for anyone in the garden. It was unlikely, though possible, someone had gone into the house without him noticing.

There was no one in the garden, but as he got closer to the house he saw it was empty inside. *Shit.* The bitch had moved.

He peered through the kitchen window and saw gaps between the units where appliances should be. They'd definitely gone. He went to the large sash window which opened onto a back reception room and pushed it up. Someone forgot to lock it. That was typical as well. The number of houses he'd gotten into because people forgot to thumb the locks on their windows…

Lance pushed it all the way open and climbed inside. He'd come this far and might as well have a look about, just in case.

He walked around downstairs aimlessly, imaging the bitch and her family in the kitchen, eating dinner together. Or watching TV in the living room. Upstairs in the bedroom, he imagined her sleeping, imagined her fucking that other woman she lived with. Now she was sitting in her nice new house, while he couldn't even go back to his flat because the police were looking for him. It made him angry. All she had to do was fucking represent him at that sham trial—it was her job, after all. Instead she sat there all snooty and told him she couldn't represent him when she knew he'd committed the crime and wouldn't plead guilty.

She was happy to take his money, though, wasn't she? Happy to bleed him dry then hang him out to dry. Fucking bitch. That's what you got for hiring a woman. His mates warned him, teased him she was probably on the rag when she'd binned him off. Instead of a decent brief, he got some court-appointed arsehole because the bitch had taken all his money, and he couldn't afford a new barrister.

No one shafted Lance Sherry. Especially not some jumped up bitch who shouldn't even be doing a man's job anyway. When he caught up with her, she'd regret turning him down.

Catching up with her was going to be more difficult now that she'd moved. Lance sighed. Why couldn't life be easy?

He went back downstairs to the kitchen. Sometimes people left things behind like bits of post or cards. He riffled through the drawers, not holding out much hope.

Lance blew out a breath in frustration. Fuck. Nothing. It was too much to hope for, anyway. Too convenient that there would be some clue as to where they'd gone. Now what?

Then he saw it. Propped up by the oven. Lance snatched up the envelope and tore it open. *Bingo.* A letter from the post office confirming the bitch's mail redirect service. Her new address was included at the bottom. Lance grinned and stuffed the letter in his pocket. It looked like luck was on his side after all.

He climbed back out the window and pulled it shut behind him. He couldn't lock the garden gate, but it wasn't a problem. The new owners would just think someone forgot to close it. The lock wasn't broken or anything.

Lance walked back out onto the street and set off down the road, whistling to himself. *Found you bitch. Going to fuck you then kill you.*

CHAPTER NINE

S adie was exhausted. They'd spent most of the afternoon unpacking boxes and putting the kids' bedroom furniture together. They'd just finished their own bed frame and were pulling on the mattress.

Sadie flopped onto it as soon as it was in place and closed her eyes. She felt it sag as Fin lay down beside her. She thought about all the other boxes they had yet to unpack, and she groaned.

"Shall I give you a massage?" Fin asked, rolling onto her side, hand on Sadie's stomach.

Sadie grinned. "I know how your *massages* always end up, and I'm too bloody tired."

Fin chuckled. "Honest, just a nice massage."

"Yes, but I'll get horny and want to have sex."

"And I shall rebuff your advances."

"Then I'll get cranky."

"And I'll give in." Fin sighed dramatically. "I'll get the sheets for the bed."

"No, I'll get them. I don't know which ones I want yet." Sadie stood up and her muscles protested.

"Does it matter?"

Fin looked confused and Sadie laughed.

"Yes. Besides, you always choose the green sheet and a duvet cover that doesn't match. Where did you put them?"

Fin rolled onto her back and sat up. "I think in the room by the kids' bathroom."

"Okay. Why don't you go and shower? I may join you in a minute."

"I thought you were too tired for sex."

"I changed my mind. And it's your conjugal duty to service me whenever I want it," she joked. She heard Fin still laughing as she walked into the bathroom.

She opened the door to the bedroom where Fin stacked the boxes and sighed. There really were loads of them. How did they manage to accumulate so much stuff? And how did they fit it all in that small three-bedroom terraced house?

Sadie shivered from the cold. Did Fin leave the window open in here? She pushed a few boxes aside to reveal the sash window behind. It was closed. Strange. It definitely felt draughty, but she supposed that was old houses for you. Old houses with knackered heating systems. Even though the previous owners did a lot of cosmetic work on the place, they'd neglected to update the heating or any of the electrics where they didn't have to. Sadie thought it was silly. Surely they were the first things you'd get fixed?

It was certainly the first thing they were going to do once they'd saved some cash and she went back to work. She'd decided to start looking for work soon, now that the idea of it didn't bring on a panic attack. She'd talked to Fin about the idea of going into family law—specifically child protection cases. The more she thought about it, the more sense it made to her. There wouldn't be as much money in it, or probably enough prestige for her father, but it meant she would be making a difference. She'd be helping people who deserved it—not lowlifes like Lance Sherry. She still believed everyone deserved representation despite what they might have done, but she just didn't want to be the person doing it any more.

Sadie shivered again and felt goosebumps rise on her arms. She opened the box marked *master bed sheets* and pulled out whatever came to hand. She had the sudden urge to get out of this room as quickly as possible.

As she turned to leave, the door slammed shut. It looked like someone pulled it from the other side which was odd. When she went to open it, she realized there was no door handle on this side. Behind her, a hissing noise started up.

Fin turned off the shower. She guessed Sadie changed her mind about joining her. For the first few months after the attack, Sadie understandably hadn't wanted sex. Fin didn't push or pressure her, but she knew Sadie felt bad about it. Before, they'd had a pretty active sex life for a couple with two kids under six.

Lately, she'd started getting a bit friskier, and Fin thought they were on the way to getting back to normal. The nightmares had also calmed down quite a bit, and Sadie was only seeing her psychologist once a week now, instead of twice. She'd joined an online support group too, which seemed to be helping.

Fin towelled off and put on her pyjamas. She frowned when she went back into the bedroom and saw the bed unmade and no sign of Sadie. Perhaps she'd gone to check on one of the kids or decided to make a cup of tea. Sometimes Sadie took a hot drink to bed with her. Fin couldn't drink caffeine after five because she wouldn't sleep, but it didn't seem to affect Sadie at all.

Fin waited a bit longer before going to look for her. She stood at the bottom of the stairs to their bedroom and listened. The house was silent.

Fin walked down to the kids' bedrooms and looked in. They were both sleeping soundly. She came back into the hall and noticed the door to the spare room was shut. That was where Sadie went to get the sheets for the bed. She turned the handle and stepped inside.

Sadie lay on the floor in the middle of the room. She wasn't moving.

Fin dropped to the floor and touched her face. She was warm, thank God. Fin felt for her pulse and found it was nice and strong. It looked like she'd fainted—maybe she'd had a panic attack? Sadie hadn't had one for a while, but maybe something triggered her.

"Sadie? Babe?" Fin said, stroking her face. "Sadie?"

She heard a groan and Sadie opened her eyes.

"Hey, babe. You fainted. Are you—"

Sadie gasped and sat up. Her eyes were wild and she looked terrified.

"Hey, hey." Fin pulled her into her arms. She was trembling. "It's okay, it's okay. You just fainted."

"No, no." Sadie struggled out of her arms and stood up, swaying on her feet. Fin grasped her arms gently to stop her from falling. "We have to get out of here, Fin. There's a gas leak."

"What?" Fin hadn't seen her like this before. Was she hallucinating? What the hell was going on. "No, Sadie. You're fine. *We're* fine. Look at me." Fin held Sadie's face between her hands and forced her to look in her eyes. "There's no gas leak, babe. I had it all checked before we moved in. There's a carbon monoxide alarm next to the boiler. We're fine."

"There was gas, coming through there." Sadie pointed up to one of the weird vents on the internal wall. "I watched the air ripple with it. And I couldn't get out. Why isn't there a fucking door handle on this side?"

Sadie searched Fin's eyes, but it looked like her terror was giving way to anger. Fin thought that was good.

"It's an old house—the handle probably fell off. I think you fainted and then…I don't know, maybe had a bad dream? Is that possible?"

"Maybe," Sadie conceded.

"Let's go upstairs to bed. I'll put the sheets on, and we can go to sleep. Okay?"

"Okay."

Sadie let Fin lead her out of the room.

Upstairs, she went in the bathroom while Fin put the sheets on. Under ordinary circumstances she would have ragged on Sadie about picking the green bottom sheet. Fin sighed. She cursed that bastard Lance Sherry for what he'd done to them.

CHAPTER TEN

Sadie stood beneath the shower spray with her face upturned. She was less shaky now. She felt like an idiot, babbling to Fin about gas coming through the vent in the wall. She must have been hallucinating. Oh well, she guessed it was something to talk to the psychologist about on Wednesday.

She could remember the door closing and not being able to get out because there was no handle inside. It must have triggered a panic attack, and then she imagined the room filling up with gas and fainted. Poor Fin. Sadie felt bad she'd had to cope with her meltdowns these last few months. Especially when they both thought things had improved. Fin never complained, though, and Sadie was surprised at how patient she was.

Fin was always great with the kids, but Sadie hadn't realized her patience would run to Sadie as well. She was lucky—other partners would have bailed by now or at least been thinking about it, she was sure.

Sadie shut the shower off and grabbed a towel. She went back into the bedroom where Fin was already under the covers with her eyes closed.

She slipped in beside her and Fin rolled towards her. "You all right, babe?" she asked, pulling Sadie into her arms. "Mmm, you smell nice." Fin nuzzled her hair and sighed.

"I'm okay. How are you?" Sadie asked.

Fin opened her eyes and looked down. "I'm good. We'll put a handle on the inside of that door tomorrow. I can only imagine how it felt being trapped in there."

That was probably it, Sadie thought. Before, she would have banged on the door and shouted for Fin to let her out. Now, the sense of being trapped—trapped like that night Lance Sherry pinned her against a wall with a knife to her throat—made her freak out and faint. Sadie wanted her life back. She was so sick of feeling like a victim.

She turned in Fin's arms and ran her hand down Fin's side. Face-to-face, she pressed her lips to Fin's and deepened the kiss. She moved her hand lower and cupped Fin outside her pyjama bottoms.

"What are you doing?" Fin pulled back.

"Shh. I'm claiming my conjugal rights."

Fin didn't laugh as she hoped.

"Sadie, you don't have to do this."

Sadie squeezed, then began using her palm to massage Fin. "I want to. I want to feel normal again."

Fin grasped her wrist gently, stilling the movement. "You are normal, babe."

"I want to feel like myself again. Let me, Fin."

Fin let go and Sadie moved her hand beneath Fin's pyjama bottoms. Fin groaned when she slipped one finger either side of her clit and began to stroke.

She claimed Fin's mouth. Her tongue pushed inside and matched the rhythm of her hand. In and out, back and forth. Fin's hips began to grind against Sadie's fingers. Her breathing got deeper and more ragged. She tried to move Sadie's fingers to where Sadie knew she needed them to come.

Sadie stopped. "Not yet, Fin."

"Sadie."

"Shh. Hang on."

Sadie slid down the bed, taking Fin's bottoms with her, then positioned herself between Fin's legs. Fin looked down at her with half-lidded eyes and grinned lazily. Sadie smiled back at her before she took Fin in her mouth and began to lick. Fin didn't last long, she noted smugly. She never did when Sadie went down on her. With a few strokes of her tongue against Fin's clit, Fin bucked against her and came.

Sadie came back up and lay on top her. Fin gripped Sadie's hips and began to grind their pelvises together. She reached between their bodies, and Sadie moaned as Fin's fingers entered her. She sat up and leaned back to take them deeper. Fin came up with her, pulled her T-shirt off, and began to suck on Sadie's nipples. It always drove her straight to the brink of orgasm when she did that. She felt Fin's fingers curl inside her, and then the heel of her hand brushed against Sadie's clit.

Sadie pushed down hard on Fin's hand and came hard, wetness soaking her thighs. She leaned in to Fin, her face between her shoulder and neck, and sighed. After all these years together, they knew each other's bodies inside out. Having small children was also a good motivator for learning how to make each other come quickly.

"What are you smiling about? I can feel you against my neck," Fin asked.

"I was just thinking about how well you make me come."

Fin laughed. "I'm still inside you. Want me to go again?"

Sadie gasped as Fin pumped her fingers, once, twice. The gasp turned to a groan as she began to stroke inside Sadie again. "Definitely," she whispered.

Fin woke with her front pressed to Sadie's back. They'd fallen asleep naked. Recently, Lucy was in the habit of climbing into their bed sometime around three—Fin could never tell exactly because she was like a ninja, and Fin only woke when she felt bony little knees pressed against the small of her back.

She rolled away from Sadie and reached down for her pyjama bottoms and top. Sadie was fast asleep and buck naked. Fin got up and went over to the suitcase by the window. It was no good—she couldn't see anything in the dark. She pulled aside the curtain to let in a little light to see by. She saw something move out of the corner of her eye. Fin peered out of the window, letting the curtain fall across her back. There it was again, over by the trees which lined their property.

Fin's first thought was Lance Sherry had found them. Then she realized the figure was much too small for a man. Her heart triple timed. Lucy. Had Lucy somehow gotten outside?

"Sadie, Sadie." Fin shook her awake. She groaned and tried to go back to sleep. "Babe, you need to wake up. It's Lucy."

Sadie's eyes flew open and she sat straight up. "What's happened?"

"There's someone outside—it might be Lucy. I'm going out there. Can you check her room?"

Sadie jumped up and ran from the room while Fin went in the opposite direction, towards the stairs.

"What's going on. Why are you naked, Mummy?" came Liam's sleepy voice behind her. Fin didn't wait to hear the rest of the conversation as she reached the bottom of the stairs. As she got to the front door, Sadie's voice came from above.

"Fin, it's not Lucy out there. She's asleep in bed."

"Okay." Fin felt a rush of relief. But if it wasn't Lucy, it was someone else's child, and she needed to go and look. "I'm going to see who it is."

Footsteps behind her made her turn around. Sadie was pulling on a dressing gown. "I'm coming with you."

Fin nodded and they headed outside.

"How do you know it's a child?" Sadie asked as they crossed the lawn towards the trees.

"It's small and it moves like a kid, you know?"

Sadie nodded.

Kids had a fluidity of movement that people lost somewhere on the way to adulthood.

"Sadie, maybe you should go back. You must be freezing in that dressing gown."

They approached the trees and Fin scanned them, hoping to see the child again.

"I'm okay. I don't want you out here on your own."

Something moved in the trees, going in the direction of the property line. "Hey!" she called out. Fin turned to Sadie. "You're barefoot, babe, go back inside."

Fin went into the trees, following the child. She didn't hear Sadie behind her and hoped she'd headed back to the house. She still wasn't doing too well with being out at night, and Fin was concerned she'd have another panic attack.

The woods thinned out slightly as she approached the fence dividing their property from their neighbour's. She saw the child again and called out, but it turned and ran. Fin started to give chase, and then she was falling.

Sadie changed into tracksuit bottoms and a sweatshirt—the house was freezing. Lucy hadn't woken at all, but Liam wouldn't go back to bed until Fin came home. They sat in the kitchen and waited.

Sadie didn't want to leave Fin alone, but she hadn't thought to put on shoes, and being out in the dark like that made her chest tight, and she feared another panic attack. She'd come back inside and called the local police station who were sending a car out. What on earth was a child doing out alone at this time? She hadn't seen it herself, but Fin was adamant it was running around out there in the middle of the night.

Last year, Sadie was home with the children alone one Saturday because Fin had to work. She'd left them outside in the garden to go in and get a drink. When she came out, Lucy had managed to let herself out of the back gate and was most of the way down the passage and into the street. Sadie understood how that could happen with a determined child, but all the same...

She heard the front door open and stood. Liam was out of the kitchen and running into the hall. Sadie followed him.

"Fin! What happened to you?"

She was covered in mud and appeared to be limping. Fin looked up from Liam's worried face and smiled sheepishly.

"I had a run in with a ditch. I'm fine. Really."

"Why did you run into the ditch?" Liam asked and Fin ruffled his hair.

"It wasn't intentional, believe me. It was dark and I took a misstep. You should be in bed."

"He wanted to make sure you were okay. Did you find the child?"

"No." Fin winced. "I'm going to get some ice. I think I twisted my ankle. Night, mate." She hobbled off into the kitchen.

Sadie took Liam back upstairs to bed. While she was tucking him in, his eyes began to droop and close as he fell asleep. She leaned over and kissed his forehead.

"Sweet dreams, darling," she whispered.

His eyes opened and stared intently into hers. "Mummy, he's coming."

Sadie flinched. She tried to stay calm. "Who, Liam?"

But Liam was asleep again—if he had even woken up in the first place. Sadie ran a shaky hand through her hair and stood. *He's coming.* Did Liam mean Lance Sherry?

Liam's ability to know things before they happened was unnerving. It was never anything major—he'd tell them someone was at the door, and a moment later the bell would ring. Now and again, though, he would say something that sent shivers up Sadie's spine. Usually it was times like now, when he was asleep or, at least, on the way to being asleep. Sometimes, the things he said meant nothing, and sometimes they did. She hoped this was one of those times it meant nothing.

❖

Liam woke up to the sensation of warmth flooding his pyjama bottoms. *Oh no!* He scrambled out of bed, flicked on the light, and threw back his duvet cover to avoid getting pee on it. His pyjamas were soggy and cold and beginning to itch, so he took them off and hung them over the chair.

Liam felt like a stupid baby. Even Lucy didn't wet the bed any more. He knew his parents wouldn't mind, but they would want to know why, and Liam didn't want to tell them about the dream. He had an idea lately, that if he didn't tell anyone about his bad dreams, then the bad man couldn't get out of them and hurt people. It was like the opposite of when you made a birthday wish—if you didn't tell about the bad dream, then it didn't come true.

Liam went to the bathroom and washed himself to get rid of the pee. He took a clean pair of pyjama pants from the cupboard. He decided to leave his bottoms to dry on the chair and keep the duvet off the bed so the sheet would dry too. Hopefully his parents wouldn't notice he'd wet the bed.

On his way back to his bedroom, Liam heard the click of a door as it opened. The sound came from downstairs. Maybe one of his parents was up? He crept along the hall and peered over the banister and saw the basement door was open and a light was on inside. Liam was scared. He didn't think it was his parents down there. His legs itched to run back into his bedroom, until he heard a giggle. Lucy.

Why was Lucy in the basement? Mum had told them they weren't to go down there alone because it was dangerous. Lucy never listened, though—she did whatever she wanted.

Liam went down the stairs. Lucy was a snot, but he didn't want her to get hurt. At the top of the basement steps, he called out to her in a whisper, so he wouldn't wake his parents.

She giggled again but didn't answer. Liam was annoyed. She was such an idiot. "Lucy," he hissed and took two steps down. He didn't want to go all the way into the basement because he wasn't allowed.

Lucy still didn't answer. "I'm telling if you don't come up right now." He went down further, so now he was about halfway down the steps. He glanced behind him guiltily, expecting one of his parents to catch him. They always seemed to be there when he did something he wasn't supposed to.

Liam crouched down and peered through the banister rails into the basement below. He could make out Lucy standing in her pyjamas. It looked like she was speaking to someone because she was nodding her head. "Lucy." He tried again.

This time she turned around and smiled at him. "Liam, look, it's Koosh." She pointed at something Liam couldn't see. It made him scared nonetheless.

"There's no one there, and we aren't allowed down here. Come up now."

Lucy shook her head. "We playing."

"I'm telling on you."

Lucy frowned at Liam. "You made him go away now."

Liam still couldn't see who she was talking to, but he had a bad feeling about it. "Please, Lucy. Before—"

Behind him, the basement door clicked shut.

Sadie sat up in bed. She felt like she hadn't been asleep for more than half an hour. Something woke her. Her first thought was of Lance Sherry before she pushed it away. Of course it wasn't Lance Sherry—he didn't know where they lived and the house was alarmed. Nonetheless…it wouldn't hurt to check. The alarm box was just inside the basement door and had a read-out to show which parts of the house were armed. She'd have a look just to put her mind at rest. Sadie pushed the covers aside and got up.

At the bottom of the stairs she could see light shining from under the basement door. That was odd. She could have sworn she'd turned it off on the way to bed. Sadie turned the handle, but the door wouldn't budge. She pushed against it with more force, but it was jammed. Sadie rattled the handle in frustration and pushed again. From the other side, she heard crying. *Liam.*

"Liam? Are you in there?"

She heard footsteps running up the stairs towards her. "Mummy! Mummy, we're stuck."

Sadie leaned her ear against the door. "How did you get in there?" She rattled the handle again. "The door's jammed. Did you lock it from that side?"

"No. It closed, and then I couldn't get it open again. Please let us out. I'm scared."

"Hang on, darling." Fin must have some kind of tool in her workshop Sadie could use to bash the door. As she turned away, she heard a click and it swung open.

Liam came charging through and into her arms. He was shaking and crying. Sadie held him close and stroked his sweaty head. "Hey, hey. It's okay, darling. The door just got stuck, that's all."

He buried his face in her stomach and continued to cry. Lucy ambled out after him, seemingly unaffected by the whole thing.

Sadie reached out with one arm as Lucy went to walk by her. "Lucy? Are you okay?"

"Yes," she said. "We was just playing."

"Why were you and Liam playing in the basement when we asked you not to go down there?" she asked.

"Sorry, Mummy," she said.

"It's late, and you need to be in bed. We'll talk about this in the morning. Liam?" Sadie held him out at arm's length. "Did you hear me?"

He nodded and wiped his nose on his pyjama sleeve.

"Come on then, it's late."

Sadie decided she would put a bolt on the outside of the basement door tomorrow. High enough so the children couldn't reach.

She walked them back up to bed.

CHAPTER ELEVEN

Fin rolled onto her side, dislodging Lucy who squealed in protest. She clambered back on and began that irritating tapping on Fin's nose again. Fin felt Lucy's breath on her face as she leaned in close.

"Mama-mama-mama-mama," she said in time with each tap. Fin tried not to laugh.

In a flash, she rolled onto her back and caught Lucy, bringing her close and blowing a loud raspberry on her neck. Lucy screamed and flailed her arms, laughing.

"For crying out loud, you two," came Sadie's muffled voice from beneath the duvet. "Give it a rest."

Fin gave Lucy a mock scowl. "That was your fault," she whispered.

Lucy giggled. "No, *your* fault."

"I'm serious." Sadie did sound serious.

Fin swung Lucy up into her arms and got out of bed, relieved her ankle felt fine after last night's fall. "Come on, let's go and get some breakfast before we wake the monster."

"Mummy's a monster! Mummy's a monster," Lucy shouted.

A pillow sailed past Fin's head as she ducked out of the room.

Downstairs, Liam was sitting at the kitchen table looking at one of his dinosaur magazines.

"Hi, mate." Fin kissed his head as she put Lucy on a chair next to him. "How long have you been up?"

Liam shrugged. "A while."

Fin put the kettle on to boil and found two bowls for cereal. "I thought we'd pop into the town today—Lucy, the bowl doesn't go on your head."

"Okay," Liam replied.

Fin looked at him, but he wouldn't take his eyes off the magazine. She knew he wasn't reading it because most of the words were still too difficult for him. "Want to tell me what's up?" She shook out some cereal into the bowls and added milk.

Liam shrugged.

"Is it about last night?" she asked.

Liam remained silent. Fin made her cup of coffee and sat at the table. "I'm not a mind reader, Liam. I can't help if you don't tell me what's wrong."

"I don't like this house."

He said it so quietly, Fin had to lean forward to hear him. "Why don't you like the house?"

He shrugged. Liam shrugged a lot.

Fin sighed and rubbed her eyes. They felt grainy and sore from lack of sleep. The police had come by about two in the morning to say they couldn't find the child. She and Sadie spent another twenty minutes giving statements. It was after three before they got to bed, and now she was up again at six thirty.

She tried again. "Is it because you aren't near your friends any more?"

"It's the *house*. I don't like the *house*."

"Why?"

"It's weird."

"The house is weird?"

"I don't like the house," he said again.

Fin took a moment and sipped her coffee. "Look, I know it's a big adjustment moving house. And before, living with Granny and Grandad. You'll get used to it, though. You'll make new friends and we'll all be happy here. I promise."

Liam stood up and pushed his chair back. The legs squealed along the tiled floor. "You don't understand." He picked up his magazine and walked out.

Christ. Sometimes it was like dealing with a sixteen-year-old instead of a six-year-old. Fin reached over and brushed cereal out of Lucy's hair.

Lance Sherry saw the problem immediately. The bitch's new house was down a quiet, narrow lane. He'd driven all the way down to where it dead-ended and back again. Most likely anyone who saw him would think he was lost. He couldn't risk driving down again, though. People noticed strange cars on roads like this. Some busybody neighbour, or maybe even the bitch herself. He'd almost panicked when he thought he saw someone looking at him from one of the upstairs windows. It looked like they were waving him in. Strange. Turned out to be a trick of the light, thank God.

He would have to find another way of scouting out the place. The area was surrounded by fields and a small bunch of trees too small to be called a wood. He could come at the house through the fields and watch from the trees, he guessed. It wasn't ideal—the old house was ideal—but he didn't have much choice.

Lance indicated and turned back onto the main road. The next time he came here, the bitch would die. Maybe he'd do her little family as well, teach her a lesson for moving somewhere which made it so difficult to stalk her. He laughed at his own joke.

Sadie was in the spare bedroom with the boxes, trying to unpack and sort them. Fin slunk off a while ago after making an excuse about going to fill in the ditch she fell in last night. Sadie didn't blame her—these boxes were a bloody nightmare.

The amount of absolute junk they'd decided to keep hold of was unbelievable. The annoying thing was, most of it was hers.

She'd been a bit wary about coming back in here, particularly when there was no handle on the inside. She'd dragged several of the heaviest boxes over to prop the door open. Liam was taking a nap, and Lucy was playing in her bedroom directly opposite this one, where she could keep an eye on her. Sadie watched her now, cramming the plastic unicorns she was obsessed with into a doll's house she'd pulled all the windows and doors off of.

Lucy was talking to herself, and Sadie smiled. She turned back to the box in front of her and pulled out a pile of electricity bills from 2004. Why had she kept these? What was wrong with her?

"Mummy?"

Sadie looked up to see Lucy had come into the room. "Yes, darling?"

"Can we play monster?" she asked.

Monster was a game Fin invented and the children loved it. It was basically hide-and-seek, except Fin clomped around the house and roared when she found them. "I'm a bit busy right now. Maybe Liam will play when he wakes up."

"No. Can *we* play monster? Me and Koosh?"

"Who?"

"*Koosh.*" Her little brow furrowed and she pursed her lips to pronounce the word properly.

Sadie frowned. "Lucy, who is Koosh?"

"My friend. We were playing unicorns, and now he wants to play monster. Can we?"

Lucy's last imaginary friend was a few months ago, but in the past couple of weeks she'd seemed to have forgotten all about him. It looked like he was back and now called Koosh. Usually she named them after cartoon characters or children from school.

"Okay, fine. But play up here where I can see you."

"We will." Lucy ran out and Sadie went back to sorting through old bills and bank statements.

❖

Fin stepped into the ditch. It wasn't as deep as she remembered it from last night, and on closer inspection didn't appear to be a ditch at all. It sloped down on one side and ended at a trapdoor which was partially covered by weeds and grass that had grown up where it hadn't been used in a long time. When she fell into it last night, she must have kicked some of it away, because part of an old wooden door with a rusted metal handle stuck up out of the ground.

Fin wondered if it was an access point to an old sewer, but that wouldn't make any sense, because the sewerage ran beneath the lane at the front of the house. This must be something else.

She used the spade she'd brought with her to clear away the grass and weeds, revealing a plain wooden door set into the earth. She reached down and lifted it, surprised at how heavy it was. The door groaned and squealed in protest as she pulled it back and released the smell of damp earth and rotten vegetation.

Fin turned on the torch built in to her phone and shone it into the hole. A set of wooden steps led down and illuminated a sodden dirt floor. Because of the angle of the steps, she couldn't see beyond the floor without going down.

She tested the first step, and it seemed to hold her weight without much trouble, though it did groan. She was reluctant to go any further in case the steps were rotten. She could go back up to the house and get a stepladder. That was probably the safest bet. The only problem was if Sadie saw her, she'd probably try to rope her into helping with the boxes. If she told Sadie about the trapdoor, she'd want to come down and look with her, and for some reason, Fin wanted to investigate it on her own. Sadie didn't even like the house. It was Fin who'd found the place and fallen in love with it, so she should be the one to discover all its nooks and crannies and secret places.

Fin pulled the trapdoor closed and kicked some dirt over it to cover it up again. Maybe she could persuade Sadie to take the kids into town this afternoon on her own. That would give Fin plenty of time to have a look around down there.

❖

Liam opened his eyes. He'd been dreaming about the bad man again, except this time, the bad man's face changed and became another man. The new man was just as bad. He was in the basement last night when the door shut, and Liam couldn't get out. Lucy laughed but Liam didn't think it was funny. She thought it was just a game, but Liam knew better. The new bad man didn't like children at all. Liam didn't think he liked anyone, really.

Liam got out of bed and walked over to the window. He looked out and saw his mum walking back across the lawn. The new bad man was walking next to her. He was whispering something in her ear. Liam was scared.

CHAPTER TWELVE

F in waved to Sadie, who was sitting at the kitchen table on the phone, and went to the sink to wash her hands. It sounded like Sadie was talking to Rachel. Rachel was keen to come down and see the place, and from what Fin overheard, it sounded like she was badgering Sadie again. Fin liked Rachel well enough, and she seemed to be a good friend to Sadie. But there was something about her that always put Fin on edge, a feeling she maybe looked down on Fin and thought Sadie could do better. That maybe *she* would be better for Sadie. Fin thought she still carried a torch for her wife. Unlike Treven, Rachel never said anything, but Fin wondered what she told Sadie when Fin wasn't around.

Fin dried her hands on a tea towel and got a bottle of water from the fridge. She hadn't realized how thirsty she was until she took a sip.

"How did it go?" Fin turned at the sound of Sadie's voice.

"Okay. Was that Rachel on the phone?"

"Yes. She keeps on about coming down and seeing our new place." Sadie bit her lip.

"What?" Fin asked and sat down at the table.

"I invited her for tomorrow evening. For dinner."

Fin sighed. They really weren't ready for guests. "We haven't unpacked all the kitchen stuff yet, and there's no food to cook."

Sadie leaned over and grinned. "How about if you give me the list, and I'll go to the supermarket for you?"

Fin remained silent.

"And I'll unpack the kitchen?" Sadie upped her offer.

Still, Fin didn't speak.

"Okay, *fine*. I'll also do the dishwasher for a week."

Fin laughed. "Deal. I'll invite Rose and her new girlfriend Janey as well."

Sadie shook her head. "You're a negotiating genius."

"Not really. You're just a bad one." Fin jumped up and avoided Sadie's swipe. On the way out of the kitchen, she heard Sadie call to her that the electrician was due this afternoon to fit the chandelier in the kitchen. Fin rolled her eyes. The bloody thing was monstrous, and Fin hated it. For some reason, Sadie, who was not generally given to such ornate tastes, loved it and insisted it was going up in the kitchen. Fin supposed it would look better there than it had in the old house.

Sadie reached into the shower cubicle and turned the spray on full. The room quickly steamed up and fogged the glass enclosure. She stepped inside and sighed as the hot water soothed her aching muscles. Both she and Fin worked hard today shifting and unpacking boxes, and she'd much rather be curling up on the sofa with Fin and a bottle of wine tonight instead of entertaining guests. Still, it would get Rachel off her back for a while.

She massaged shampoo into her hair as the bathroom door clicked open.

"Hello, darling," she called out. "I found one of the wine boxes in the spare room. Will you pick a couple to go with dinner?"

Fin didn't answer her. She must have left again. Sadie loved this shower. She could stay in here forever with the water beating down from the double showerheads. Heaven. It was probably the only thing she loved about the house, if she was honest. She was trying her best to like it because Fin was so in love, but there was something about it which made Sadie uncomfortable. Perhaps it was the incident on the first night when she got trapped in the spare room. Maybe that was colouring her view of the place. That must be it, because there was really nothing to dislike. The views were beautiful and the original features were lovely. All the same...there was just something about it. Something that didn't feel quite right.

Sadie switched off the shower and opened the cubicle door. The room was filled with steam and she made a mental note to open the bedroom windows to air it out, or they were in danger of getting mouldy walls. Fin thrust a towel at her—or rather Fin's arm appeared, holding the towel.

"Thanks, darling. Did you hear what I said about the wine?"

Sadie wrapped the towel around her and stepped out. Fin was gone again, which was strange because she didn't see her leave.

Back in the bedroom, there was no sign of her either. Confused, Sadie dried off and dressed.

Fin lifted the pan lid and stirred the sauce. Usually she loved to cook, but tonight it was a hassle. If she'd had her way, she and Sadie would be curled up on the sofa with wine and their books. Still, she hadn't seen Rose for a while and it would be good to meet her new girlfriend.

"That smells amazing."

Fin turned and smiled at Sadie as she came in carrying two bottles of wine. "Good shower?"

"Umm, yes. Pity you shot downstairs so fast—you could have joined me." Sadie smiled.

"What do you mean?" Fin replaced the lid on the pan and picked up the wine.

"Earlier, when you handed me my towel." Sadie's smile faltered.

"What are you going on about? I've been slaving over dinner for the last hour." Fin laughed and opened one of the bottles to let it breathe. "I don't know if Janey drinks red, so I'll grab a bottle of white from upstairs."

"Fin, wait." Sadie touched her arm.

"Are you okay, babe? You look worried."

"No, I…are you sure you didn't come upstairs?"

Fin put the wine on the table and pulled Sadie into her arms. "Promise. Maybe it was one of the kids you heard?"

"Maybe."

Fin kissed her and released her. "I need to grab that wine and then get changed."

"Okay."

"Love you."

"Love you."

❖

Sadie sat down at the kitchen table. She could have sworn Fin was in the bathroom, but she wouldn't lie about it. And if Fin didn't hand her the towel, then who did? It was so strange. She thought of Lance Sherry, and then dismissed the idea as stupid. If he'd managed to find out where they lived, why would he go to the trouble of breaking in just to hand her a towel? He wouldn't.

Now that she thought about it, she didn't actually *see* Fin pass her the towel—didn't even see her arm. The towel appeared in front of her. Perhaps it was hanging up all along and she assumed Fin gave it to her because she thought she was in the bathroom.

Sadie sighed. Maybe she wasn't all the way back to her old self, after all. First she was imagining gas leaks and now this. Sadie decided to talk to the psychologist next week about it.

CHAPTER THIRTEEN

Fin was drunk. She looked around the table and thought everyone else was too. The evening had turned out to be a lot of fun. Rose's girlfriend Janey was lovely. She was also cute, exactly Rose's type. She was tall with short red hair and warm brown eyes and Fin thought Rose seemed very happy with her—well, if the soppy grin pasted on her face was anything to go by.

Rachel was being her usual self. She'd been agitated when she first got here because she'd driven past the turn-off to the house several times without seeing it. Fin had to go out and wave her in.

Fin had burst out laughing, though, when Rachel walked into the kitchen, clocked the light fitting, and said to Sadie, "I was hoping you got rid of that terrible thing. Honestly, Sadie, I sometimes wonder if you're channelling Liberace."

That led on to a discussion of Janey's hobby. Ghost hunting. She told them she often did night-time tours of supposedly haunted houses. Fin tried not to roll her eyes, but the whole thing was bollocks. She'd watched a haunted house thing on the TV once. They'd spent the entire night filming orbs which were really just specks of dust caught in the light from the cameras.

"How do you know whether they're haunted?" Sadie asked, and Fin realized she'd zoned out.

"Usually there's previous reports of sightings or strange things going on."

"Then you all hurry down there and…what exactly?" Rachel asked.

"We have equipment to test for paranormal activity."

"You're on board with this?" Rachel sloshed her wine glass in Rose's direction. "Of course you are."

"Rachel," Sadie warned.

"I'm just asking. Fin, do you believe in all this?"

Fin wasn't sure how to answer. She didn't want to be rude to Janey and say it was all crap.

"Fin doesn't believe in anything," Rose piped up. "Do you, Fin? Even when something unexplainable and totally creepy happens."

Great. Rose was going to bring that up. Fin felt Rachel's keen eyes land on her.

"Explain, Rose," she slurred.

"I mustn't. Fin doesn't like to talk about it."

Fin poured herself more wine. "Because it was a stupid game that didn't mean anything."

"Stop talking in riddles," Rachel demanded. "Sadie, do you know what they're talking about?"

"No." Sadie shook her head. "But I'm intrigued."

"It was years ago. At a party," Fin said.

"How about I tell it? You won't give it the right gravitas." Rose reached over and drank from Fin's glass.

"You mean I won't embellish."

Rose laughed and kicked her under the table. She leaned forward and spoke to the rest of them. "We were about fifteen years old. I didn't know Fin that well, but we used to go to some of the same parties. So, one night, most people had gone home. There were about five of us left. Julie Martin, who I had a big crush on by the way, wanted to play a game."

"Julie Martin? Seriously?" Fin butted in.

"Shut up, Fin. Anyway, her older sister played it at another party and said it really worked, so we decided to give it a go. What you do is, two of you each hold two pens or whatever—sticks are fine. You touch each other's pens at the tips to make sort of train tracks. Then, you say—"

"Spirits, are you there, are you there? Spirits, are you there?" Fin said in a spooky voice and earned herself a dirty look from Rose. At least Sadie laughed.

"If the pens move, it means they are. Then you ask them questions. They go inwards for yes and outwards for no."

"So what happened when you played?" Rachel was engrossed in this story, and Fin felt sorry for her that it was going to be such a let-down.

"Nothing bloody happened," Fin said.

"A picture flew across the room and smashed the TV. Fin, you are such a party pooper," Rose complained.

"A picture *fell off* the TV and smashed," Fin corrected her.

"I still think it was the spirits." Though Rose could see she'd lost the room, she shot Fin another dirty look.

"I want to play. Sadie, do you have any pens?" Rachel asked.

"For God's sake, Rachel," Fin said. "It's nonsense—no offence, Janey."

Janey smiled. "None taken."

"Oh, come on. Let's play. It'll be fun," Rachel said.

Fin looked over at Sadie, who seemed worried. She reached over and squeezed her hand. "Okay, babe?"

Sadie nodded. "Fin's right. It's silly."

"Fine. Rose, you'll play with me? The rest of you can watch."

"Sure," Rose said.

Fin sighed and got up to find them pens.

"Let's get some mood lighting in here. Is there a dimmer for the lights?" Rachel asked.

Sadie stood up and adjusted the switch, so the kitchen was bathed in long shadows. She shivered, then felt silly. It was a stupid child's game, and it didn't mean anything, but it made her nervous. She hadn't told anyone about her experience in the bathroom and put it down to still not quite being herself. This mini séance wasn't helping matters.

"Gather round, children," Rachel said as she took her position opposite Rose, and they touched the tips of their brightly coloured pens. Fin got them from the children's craft box and Sadie almost asked her not to. She didn't want them to be tainted by whatever this was. She kept quiet though and was looking at Rachel and Rose, though she was beginning to wish she hadn't. This didn't feel right. She couldn't explain it, but she felt dread slowly building.

"Right, what is it we say?" Rachel asked Rose.

"Spirits, are you there, are you there? Spirits, are you there?"

Before they could say it again together, the pens shot inwards. Rachel laughed, delighted. Sadie glanced across at Janey who wasn't smiling at all. She looked worried.

"Was that you?" Rose asked Rachel.

Rachel shook her head. "Must be the spirits," she mocked. "Ask it a question."

"Are you a good ghost?" Rose asked.

The pens moved outwards. Rachel laughed again. "It *is* you, Rose. Stop it!"

Sadie saw Rose wasn't smiling any more, and the dread gave way to fear.

"It isn't me. Rachel, if it's you, stop, because it's not funny," Rose said.

"I'm not doing it. Gosh, it must be the ghouls!" Rachel was still finding it all hilarious. She didn't notice everyone else had stopped smiling.

"Maybe we should stop," Fin said, glancing at Sadie.

Sadie nodded. "I agree."

"Me too," Janey chipped in.

"You're all so boring." Rachel rolled her eyes. "Come on, one more question and then we can stop."

The others nodded.

Rachel asked in a dramatic voice, "Do you mean us harm?"

The lights overhead flickered. The pens slowly moved inwards. Sadie watched in horror. "Rachel, this isn't funny," she whispered.

Upstairs, a door slammed and everyone jumped. Rose dropped the pens as if they were on fire and got up quickly from her seat. The lights went out just as something touched Sadie's shoulder, and she screamed.

❖

"Sadie, for Christ's sake, it's me," Fin snapped.

She felt Sadie's shoulders sag with relief and regretted being short tempered. She turned her around and held her. "Sorry. I didn't mean to snap at you."

"Well, this is a story I'll be telling on Monday," Rachel said. She used her phone's torch to light the room. "Got any candles?"

Fin rolled her eyes. "It's probably the circuit breakers. I'll go and flick them back on."

"I'll help," said Janey.

Fin led the way to the basement. "I'm sorry about Rachel. She can be a brat sometimes."

Janey chuckled. "She's okay. Fin, can I ask a question?"

"Sure." Fin found the switch and flicked it. The lights on the ground floor came back on and she heard Rachel whoop from the other room.

"Don't take this the wrong way, but has anything else strange happened since you moved in?"

Fin bristled. "No."

"If you like, I could bring some friends—"

"Your ghost hunter friends?"

"Yes. We could set up our equipment and see if there's anything here."

"I don't think so. Look, I know you're interested in hauntings, but it's not a good idea. I don't want the kids scared—or Sadie. She's been through enough."

Janey's intelligent eyes scanned her and Fin was uncomfortable beneath the scrutiny. "Okay. If you change your mind, let me know. What just happened is worrying."

"Worrying? It was a stupid game. Rachel was probably moving the pens and the electrics in this place are dodgy."

Janey nodded and Fin could see she wasn't convinced. "I feel like there's something here. I don't think it's good."

Fin resisted the urge to roll her eyes. She liked Janey, but she didn't have the patience for this spooky nonsense. "Let's get back to the others. I think there's another bottle of wine somewhere."

Janey seemed like she wanted to say more but thought better of it. She nodded and followed Fin back into the kitchen.

Chapter Fourteen

F in was in the basement, sorting through the boxes she'd found the other day. Sadie had gone upstairs to tackle the spare room. It seemed like there was no end to this unpacking and sorting. Fin still hadn't gotten a chance to go and inspect the tunnel. If it wasn't the kids demanding her time, it was Sadie.

Fin sighed and sat back on her haunches. That wasn't fair. Of course they wanted her time—they were her family, her responsibility. Lately, though, she felt as if everything fell on her shoulders. Before Sadie's attack, Fin handled the kids and all the house stuff. It made sense, because Sadie worked longer hours and her job paid more. Since she'd quit, it seemed as though Fin was still carrying the heavier load, so that now, when all she wanted was a few hours to herself to look at the tunnel, she was down here sorting through dusty old boxes—

Hang on, this was interesting. Fin picked up a leather-bound book of some kind. She turned it over in her hands, then opened it. The pages were yellowed with age, and she traced one finger over the elegant cursive script. Her finger tingled.

She skimmed over it, realizing it was some sort of journal. The date at the top read *16th July 1888*. Fin flicked through the pages from back to front and saw on the inside page the name *Nathaniel Cushion* was written in the same elegant hand which filled the journal.

Fin was excited. This must have belonged to the man who built the house. She put it to one side to read later.

With renewed energy, Fin started to sort through the other items in the box: photos, documents, another leather-bound book which looked like a ledger rather than a journal. Near the bottom was a bundle of papers tied together. She briefly read the top one. Boring. Looked like letters from an insurance company. Perhaps Nathaniel Cushion had been some kind of insurance agent. The internet should be able to help her find out.

She was tempted to stay longer and start reading everything in the box, but she needed to get started on work. There were a couple of pieces she had to finish in a few weeks. She sighed and stood up.

❖

Fin's stomach dropped when she came out of her workshop and saw the unmarked police car pull up. She knew it was police because DC Helen Lyle was driving. The officer got out of the car, and Fin walked over to meet her.

"Have you caught him?"

The look on Helen Lyle's face said it all. "I'm sorry, no. Can we go inside and talk?"

Fin nodded. "The kids are home. I'll put a film on for them in the living room while we talk." Fin leaned the spade against the wall outside.

Helen Lyle followed Fin inside and remarked how nice the house was. Fin couldn't summon any pride and mumbled thanks. She went upstairs to where Sadie was sitting cross-legged on the floor, piles of paper around her. She looked up and smiled when she saw Fin observing her. The smile left her face when Fin didn't return it.

"Darling, what's wrong?"

"Helen Lyle is downstairs. She's come to talk to us," Fin said.

"Have they caught him?"

Fin's heart hurt at the hope in her eyes. "She says not. Where are the kids?"

"Lucy's playing monster with her new imaginary friend, and Liam's in his room."

"Let's put a film on for them while we talk."

Sadie nodded and stood. Fin held out her hand and she took it. It was cold in Fin's and trembled a little.

Downstairs, once the kids were sitting in front of the TV, Fin made tea, then sat with the other women at the table.

"We believe Lance Sherry is back in the country."

"I wasn't aware he'd left," Fin said.

Sadie's hands were clutched tightly around her mug. "How do you know he's back?"

"We picked up a friend of his last night on something unrelated. It came up that he'd lent Lance his car. We did an ANPR search—"

"That's a number plate recognition search," Sadie told Fin.

"Right. His car was spotted on CCTV near your old house."

Fin felt the rage build. She licked her lips. "He's still after Sadie then." She stood and began to pace because she couldn't sit down.

"We have no reason to believe he knows your new address, and he'll slip up at some point."

"He hasn't so far," Fin shot back.

"London alone has tens of thousands of CCTV cameras. There's no way he can go anywhere in the city—in the country, for that matter—undetected for long. After he attacked you, Ms. Tate, we have strong evidence to show he went to Spain. We caught him coming off a ferry from France at Dover using a false passport. We used CCTV to track him to South London, where he lives. We've got his picture out to every traffic patrol and every station. We will find him sooner rather than later."

To Fin's surprise, Sadie reached over and took Helen Lyle's hand. "Thank you. I know you will."

"So what do we do in the meantime?" Fin asked, feeling calmer. If Sadie wasn't going to flip out, then nor would she.

"With your permission, I'd like to put a car outside your house on the lane. I see you've had an alarm installed, and I'd like you to make sure you use that every night. Like I said, we don't have any reason to believe he knows where you live now. But it's best to be cautious."

"You said you caught him hanging around our old house?" Fin asked.

"Yes. We checked it out, and there was no forced entry. He was probably having a look and realized it was empty and that you'd moved."

"Darling, sit down. You're making me dizzy," Sadie said.

Fin pulled out the chair next to her and slumped into it. "Maybe it would be a good idea if you and the kids went on holiday for a bit."

Sadie looked at her like she'd gone mad. "What? No."

"Sadie, think about it." Fin grasped her hands. They were still so cold. "You'll be out of the way—you'll be safe."

"And how will we pay for it, Fin? Magic beans?"

"Your dad wanted to give you money a while ago. He can lend it to us for this."

Sadie stroked her thumb over the back of Fin's hand. "Fine. But you're coming with us."

"I can't, babe. I have to work."

"It might not be a bad idea, Ms. Tate." Helen Lyle spoke up.

"I'll think about it," Sadie said. "Like you said, he doesn't know where we live. You're posting a car at the top of the road."

"We'll let you know tomorrow," Fin said.

❖

Sadie was numb. She tried to concentrate on the box in front of her. All she could think about was Lance Sherry.

Sherry was back, and he'd headed straight for their old house. If that didn't signal his intentions, nothing did. He wasn't finished with her, and until he was caught, he never would be. Sadie didn't try to understand his vendetta against her because there wasn't much to understand. She'd met him, she'd sat across a desk from him, while he'd calmly discussed stabbing someone in cold blood. Sadie had watched his face as he recounted the incident, and she saw not a flicker of remorse. On the contrary, he seemed to enjoy it. That was when she told him he couldn't plead not guilty. He truly didn't understand why she couldn't defend his not guilty plea in court.

She was sure there was a medical term for him. A neat little box to put him in that made him seem less malevolent. Except Sadie knew differently. Lance Sherry was the thing that lived under the bed. His was the hand that reached out in the night and grabbed your ankle if it wasn't under the duvet.

Lance Sherry was a monster, and she had brought him into her children's lives. If she hadn't been sure before, she was sure now. There was no way she was going back to her old job.

For the first time in her life, Sadie felt despair. She hated this house, and she hated Lance Sherry, and between the two of them, she was trapped.

Fin brushed off the incident the other night as faulty electrics. She refused to see anything else. Sadie sensed a badness in this place. She felt silly for thinking it, and her rational mind kept telling her it was only the stress of Sherry making her feel this way. Another part, the primitive part, nodded its head in agreement and whispered to her to run, get away from here.

Sadie pulled out a dog-eared book she vaguely remembered packing away. She turned it over in her hands. It was an old Ray Bradbury novel.

"*Something Wicked This Way Comes.*" She read the title out loud. Then she laughed. Then she started to cry.

Lance Sherry looked out the window. The man was still there, sitting on the wall and watching him. The first time Lance saw him, he thought he'd lost his mind. The bloke was dressed like something out of a period drama. He was the same man who stood in the window at the bitch's house. Lance wondered about that. He wondered how he knew it was the same man, when he thought it was a trick of the light before. Somehow, he *knew* it was the same person, the same way he *knew* the man didn't mean him any harm.

Lance rubbed his eyes and glanced at the coffee table behind which was littered with takeaway containers and empty vodka bottles. Maybe he was losing it after all. He certainly hadn't felt like himself since he came back from that house. He couldn't sleep and he was restless. He had dreams. Weird dreams that left him terrified and exhilarated at the same time.

Lance couldn't tell anybody about the man on the wall because what if he wasn't really there? What if he was? Lance sensed the man wanted him for something. He got a feeling of rightness and comfort when he looked at him.

Now the man was smiling. His long-fingered hand was outstretched as he beckoned Lance outside. Lance wanted to go out there. Had an almost paralysing need to go out there and see this man because he would make everything all right again. Yeah, he wanted to help Lance. He was a friend.

Lance turned away from the window and looked for his shoes.

❖

That night, Sadie dreamed about Lance Sherry. In the dream he'd cornered her in the spare bedroom with all the boxes. The door was shut, and she couldn't open it from this side. She tried to scream for Fin, but no sound would come out. Sherry lunged at her with the knife, and she jumped back. She fell, scattering piles of old bills everywhere. He stood over her, grinning. *Going to fuck you and kill you, bitch.* He held out the knife like he was going to stab her. His face came closer and closer, and then it changed. She wasn't looking at Lance Sherry any more, though the face was still familiar to her. She couldn't place it. It was a man. He was blond and thin and his smile was cruel, but the knife was gone and that was a blessing. Above her, she heard the hiss of gas, like when you turned on the stove.

She looked at the man and his face changed again. He looked like a monster. She screamed.

"Sadie. Sadie." She woke up with Fin's arms around her. Her skin was greasy with sweat, and she was crying and gasping for air.

Fin rocked her steadily back and forth, and eventually she felt her heartbeat slow down. Fin muttered soothing words into her hair.

"I'm okay. I'm okay now," she said and sat up, pulling the duvet around her. The sweat was drying, making her cold. "I'll call my dad in the morning," she said.

"Thank you." Fin looked relieved.

Sadie nodded. "I love you."

"I love you too."

"Why? I'm a mess." It popped out before she could stop it and she saw Fin flinch.

"You aren't a mess. You're a strong, capable woman who's been through a horrible trauma, and it's still not over. That piece of shit is still out there. I wish I could kill him."

Sadie suddenly had a horrible thought. "You won't do anything stupid while we're away, will you, Fin?"

Fin didn't answer.

"Fin. Promise me you'll let the police catch him. He's dangerous. The people he's involved with are dangerous. Promise me."

"Of course I'm not going to do anything. Don't worry."

But Sadie was worried, and Fin still hadn't promised her.

"Promise me, Fin."

"Fine. Okay. I promise."

Sadie supposed that would have to do. She wasn't sure if Fin still kept in touch with people from where she used to live. Sadie knew she had a couple of uncles—her dad's brothers—who were just as horrible as Lance Sherry. As far as she knew, Fin didn't have anything to do with them any more, but that didn't mean she didn't know how to find them if she needed to.

Sadie hoped the promise she'd made meant something to her. She'd never broken one before, and Sadie prayed she wouldn't now.

She climbed out of bed and went into the bathroom.

CHAPTER FIFTEEN

Fin waved to the police parked on the lane outside the house. She'd just dropped Sadie and the kids off at the airport and missed them already. She pulled up out front of the house and sat with the engine running. This house was supposed to be their new start. It was supposed to be somewhere Sadie could feel safe and begin to heal. Instead, she was running from here too. All because that bastard Lance Sherry decided he wanted to hurt her.

She looked up at the dark windows, at her empty house, and gripped the steering wheel so hard her knuckles went white. There should be children in there, her wife. Except they were on a plane, running away from a piece of shit the world wouldn't miss if he was gone. Fin had grown up with people like him, leeches who fed off others' misery. They enjoyed making people suffer. It made their own pathetic lives seem less shit. They were like a disease, people like Lance Sherry. The only way to beat them was to play them at their own game.

Except she'd promised she wouldn't do anything do him, and she always kept her promises to Sadie. The silent, dark house seemed to mock her. If she couldn't keep her family safe, she didn't deserve to have them or this place.

Fin sighed and rubbed her eyes. She turned off the engine and got out. She'd made a promise that she'd leave this to the police.

She decided she'd give them a week to find him. After that, all bets were off.

Fin tossed and turned all night and woke up exhausted. She remembered snippets of dreams, most of them involving a long dark tunnel that seemed to go on forever and passages and stairs which led to nowhere. She sighed and checked her phone. Sadie and the kids would still be asleep, so she couldn't call them. There was a text from Rose. Maybe she'd go down to London for a visit. One of her uncles and a cousin still lived in the area, and she hadn't seen them in years. She quickly dismissed this thought because there was only one reason she would ever see them, and she'd assured Sadie she wouldn't.

Downstairs, she put the kettle on for coffee and stared out the kitchen window. She still had a fair bit to do around the house, clearing the basement and fitting a handle on the spare room door. She had the furniture from her old workshop being delivered later, and a couple of pieces she was behind on. Then there was the trapdoor she found. She wanted to check that out. At least she'd have plenty to be getting on with while Sadie and the kids were away. It would take her mind off Lance Sherry as well.

After her coffee, Fin took a torch and ladder and went back to where she'd found the trapdoor. It looked the same as she'd left it. She kicked away the dirt she covered it with and pulled on the handle. She eased the ladder down and leaned it against the side of the pit. She tested a couple of rungs and then climbed down.

Like before, it smelled of damp earth and rotten leaves. The ground was spongy beneath her feet. She shone her torch on the narrow tunnel in front of her. It was about four feet high by three feet wide and went in the direction of the house. Fin crouched and shone the torch inside. Wooden beams shored up the tunnel, and when she pulled on them, they seemed sturdy enough. She'd never been claustrophobic, but the idea of crawling through there gave her the creeps. Not to mention the idea of the tunnel caving in and trapping her down here.

She guessed it probably ran about six hundred and fifty feet or so to the house. Not too far. Should she chance it? She felt drawn to it and repulsed by it at the same time and couldn't explain why. It was just a tunnel. Probably someone had dug it as an escape route a long time ago. It might be interesting to get hold of a history of the house. Somewhere as old as this was bound to have a few interesting stories. Especially if someone needed an escape tunnel.

As she was about to stand up, she heard footsteps above her. They were quiet, as if the person didn't want to be heard. Fin froze, her mind immediately going to Lance Sherry. What if he had found them? She turned off the torch.

The footsteps stopped, and she could sense someone up there, listening. They'd probably found the trapdoor and were trying to hear if anyone was down there. Some instinct told Fin to stay quiet. She waited. The person up there waited too.

Suddenly, the ladder was pulled up and away.

The trapdoor slammed shut.

Fin tried not to panic. She left the light off in case it could be seen around the edges of the door. She waited to see if anything else would happen. When it didn't, Fin flicked the torch back on. It looked like she was going through the tunnel after all. If it had been Sherry up there, he didn't know the house, so she was confident she could get out the other side before he found it. She tried to remember if she'd locked the front door.

A horrible thought occurred to her: What if there was no other way out? What if this was a dead end like in her dreams last night? She felt sick.

I can't think like that. It won't do anyone any good. Fin got onto her hands and knees and put the end of the torch in her mouth. She crawled forward.

Sadie got Fin's voicemail again. She'd called a couple of times already. She'd slept badly—Liam kept waking up from bad dreams. Fin was usually the one who was able to get him back off to sleep, but Fin wasn't here—she was at the house. When Sadie asked him what his nightmares were about, he couldn't remember. All he could tell her was he dreamed Fin was in danger. That he'd seen her in a dark hole, and she couldn't get out. During one particularly bad one, Sadie had tried to wake him but couldn't. He suddenly sat upright in bed, gripped her arm, and said, "She found him." The way he said it scared her. It made her think of the other night back home when she'd put him to bed, and he'd pretty much said the same thing.

Sadie didn't know what to do except call Fin and make sure she was okay. Now she wasn't answering her phone, and all Sadie could think about was what Liam said. *She found him.* Did he mean Lance Sherry? Had he found out where they lived? Sadie knew she should have insisted that Fin come with them. It was so typical of Fin to think she would be okay, like she was untouchable. Sadie knew Lance Sherry, and if he couldn't get to her, he would take Fin instead.

Sadie tried to push the thoughts from her head. Tried to stop herself imagining Fin lying in a pool of blood. She got up, careful not to disturb Lucy who was laying starfish-like on the bed, and slid open the doors to the balcony. She breathed in the early morning air which was already warm. The sky was clear, and she could tell it would be another beautiful day. Sadie would take the children down to the beach, where Lucy would insist she could swim and keep making a break for the sea. Liam would want to spend hours looking at the tide pools in the rocks for little crabs and shells.

She smiled at the thought. Fin was fine, Sherry would be caught, and they'd all live happily ever after. She repeated this over and over in her head like a mantra.

Sadie stood outside for as long as she could stand it before going back inside to call Fin again.

CHAPTER SIXTEEN

The tunnel wasn't that bad. It stayed the same size all the way down, and the beams still looked sturdy despite being old. Fin could crawl on all fours and probably even crab-walk if she wanted, though crawling was easier.

It was hard to tell how long the tunnel was, but Fin guessed her estimate of six hundred and fifty feet wasn't far off. She reached the end fairly quickly, relieved to see her fear of it being a dead end didn't materialize. She stopped and sat back on her heels.

Now she had another problem—two, really. The first was getting out of this tunnel, and the second was seeing if whoever shut the trapdoor was waiting on the other side. There was an archway cut roughly into the hard-packed earth. Pushed right up against it were piles of boxes and broken furniture. The same junk that was in the basement and where Fin must now be.

There was no light down here, which didn't necessarily mean no one was in the basement with her. They could be crouching off to the side or at the top of the steps. Even if they weren't in the basement at all, if there was someone in the house, the noise of her clearing the junk out of her path would bring them running.

Fin sighed and wiped sweat out of her eyes. It had mixed with the damp earth and made some sort of nasty face mask on her skin.

Well, she couldn't wait here forever. Fin hefted the weight of the torch in her hand, figuring it might be useful if she got the chance to use it.

She sat back on her arse and used her feet to push against the junk. She'd seen it from the other side and knew it was stacked deep. The first push didn't even budge the pile. She tried again, this time not trying to do it quietly. Sweat streamed down her face and into her eyes. Her lower back and legs throbbed. It shifted a fraction of an inch.

Fin stopped to catch her breath. Her T-shirt was stuck to her back and soaked through. After a minute, she tried again. This time, she scooted around and wiggled her fingers so her hands were either side of the archway. She held on to it, and then pushed with her back against the junk. Her heels dug into the earth, and her arms acted as leverage against the heavy pile of crap. Slowly, it started to move. She pushed again, every muscle straining, her T-shirt ripped at the armpits, and she imagined herself as the Incredible Hulk. It made her laugh, even though her situation was about as funny as dysentery.

She gave one last push, and then something in the pile gave. Fin thought it sounded like a cabinet crashed to the floor. She heard other bits of furniture and boxes begin to tumble like dominoes, and then she was turning around and crab-walking out of the tunnel.

The sense of relief was huge. She took in lungfuls of the damp, musty air and brought her ruined T-shirt up to wipe the bottom over her face.

Now all she had to do was get upstairs and out of the house in one piece. In the corner, something moved.

Liam woke up screaming. Sadie ran in from the balcony to find him thrashing violently on the bed, the covers twisted around his legs.

Sadie sat beside him and leaned over, trying to hold down his arms, which were fighting off something unseen. It seemed to make things worse, so instead she gathered him into her arms.

His elbow connected with her cheekbone and she saw stars for a minute.

"Shh. Liam, you're dreaming. Shh." She rocked him like she had when he was a baby. Back and forth, back and forth, back and forth.

Slowly his thrashing became less frantic, and his body went limp. He was panting, and when she looked down his big brown eyes were glassy. Sadie reached out and ran her hand over his hair and down the back of his head. Sadie continued to rock him, staring down at his face and willing him to come back.

Behind her, she heard a sniffle. *Lucy.* She'd forgotten all about Lucy. Sadie turned her head. Lucy stood in the middle of the room. Her T-shirt had ridden up, exposing her softly rounded tummy, and she was sucking her thumb. She hadn't done that for over a year now. She wasn't crying, but her eyes were wet, darting between Sadie and Liam, and her lower lip quivered.

With one hand Sadie reached out, and Lucy ran over and climbed onto the bed.

"Liam's having a bad dream. There's nothing to be scared of. He'll be fine in a minute."

Lucy pulled her thumb from her mouth with a pop. "I want Mama," she said.

So do I. God, so do I. "I know, darling. We'll see her soon."

Liam moved in her arms and she looked down at him. He blinked slowly and struggled to sit, staying in the circle of her arms. Sadie couldn't hide her relief. "Oh, thank God. Liam, are you okay?"

He nodded, then saw Lucy and gave her a watery smile. "I had a bad dream."

"You was screaming," Lucy told him solemnly. "Woke me up."

"Sorry," he said.

"You don't need to be sorry, Liam."

"I want to go home," he said suddenly.

"We can't yet."

"We *have* to," he insisted.

"Why?"

He looked away. "Don't remember. I want to go home. I want to see Mum."

Liam crossed his arms and his chin jutted out. Sometimes he seemed so grown up, and other times, like now, Sadie was reminded he was only six. Just a baby.

She sighed and rubbed her eyes. She could feel a headache building behind her eyes. On the bedside table, her phone buzzed.

Fin.

CHAPTER SEVENTEEN

Fin walked towards the police car and signalled for them to wind down their window. She bent down and looked in.

"Did you see anyone come down here? Up to the house?" she asked.

"No. Not this way. Did something happen?" the older guy asked her.

"What about you two? Did either of you go around the back of the house?" She didn't answer his question.

"No. Ms. Claiborne, is something wrong?"

Fin wasn't sure how much to say. There was no sign of anyone in the house—she'd checked everywhere and it was locked up tight. Except for the giant bloody rat that had scurried out at her in the basement.

After finding out about Lance Sherry, she'd made sure all the windows and the back door were locked and bolted. The front door hadn't been tampered with either. If it wasn't Lance Sherry, then who had pulled up the ladder and shut her in? It didn't make any sense. If it was someone passing by, wouldn't they have called out to see who was down there?

She realized they were waiting for an answer. She was also aware of how she looked. Even now, for reasons she couldn't explain, she was reluctant to tell anyone about the trapdoor and the tunnel.

"No, no nothing's wrong."

"Are you sure? You look...umm..."

"I've been moving all the junk in the basement." It wasn't a total lie. "Years' worth of crap down there. Sorry to bother you. I'm going to make a cup of tea in a bit. I'll bring you one out."

She straightened up, hiding the wince caused by the pain in her lower back. She'd need some painkillers and a hot bath tonight, or she would feel it tomorrow.

Fin decided to check around the back of the house, at the tunnel. Just to see if the person who shut her in was still hanging around. After that, she'd head down to the basement and try to tidy up some of the mess she'd made. And cover that tunnel back up. She told herself it was in case one of the kids found it and went for a wander, but that wasn't quite the truth.

Fin took another walk around the property and couldn't find any sign of anyone. She picked up the ladder and stored it back in the shed. In the kitchen, she boiled the kettle for tea, and that was when she saw her phone. Shit, six missed calls. All from Sadie. Fin picked it up and dialled her wife.

Fin was about to hang up when Sadie answered in a rush, "Oh, Fin, thank God. Where were you? I was so worried."

"I'm sorry, babe, I was in the basement. Is everything okay? Are the kids all right?"

"They're fine. We're fine. I've been calling you since early this morning."

Fin set out three cups and tea bags for her and the officers and poured the water, the phone cradled between her shoulder and ear. "I left it in the kitchen. I didn't mean to worry you. How's it going over there?"

"Liam had a nightmare, a bad one. He's okay now," she added quickly. "Lucy's trying to catch a spider on the balcony."

Fin laughed. She closed her eyes, picturing her family. She missed them. "I miss you."

She heard Sadie's deep sigh on the other end of the phone. "We miss you too. The children want to come home."

"What? They're on holiday—off school. Why do they want to come back?"

"To see you, of course. Is there any news on...you know." Sadie lowered her voice.

"No babe. Nothing." She didn't tell Sadie about this morning. It would only worry her, and Fin didn't think it was Sherry after all. "They'll catch him soon."

"I hope so. I want to come home."

Fin felt a lump rise in her throat. "Yeah." Her voice was rough. "So, what are you up to today?"

"I'm going to start on the basement, I think. I've got some furniture being delivered from the old workshop later, and I really need to crack on with it."

"You'll be careful in the basement? There's so much stuff down there. I don't want it to fall on you—not while there's nobody around."

If only you knew. "I'll be fine. I won't touch the heavy stuff on my own. That lad from the town is coming up when the furniture arrives, so I'll get him to give me a hand with the big stuff."

"Okay then. I love you."

"I love you too."

"Do you want to speak to the children?"

"Yes, please."

Fin spoke to the kids for a bit and then Sadie again. When they finally hung up, she felt an acute loneliness she remembered from childhood. Meeting Sadie made it go away, and now it was back again. She missed her family.

She thought again how unfair it was that piece of shit Lance Sherry got to walk around without a care in the world, while her family were forced to leave their home. She felt impotent and helpless. She should be doing something, not pissing about in tunnels and basements. She had to do something.

❖

Downstairs in the basement, Fin surveyed the wreckage from her escape. A tallboy had fallen forward and smashed to pieces. A bunch of mismatched dining chairs had tumbled over, though they looked more or less in one piece.

Fin carried the plyboard over to the now exposed tunnel and held it against the archway opening. It would fit, and if she moved all the furniture and boxes back, no one would know it was there. Or be able to get through. But especially, know it was there.

She nailed the board in place, then began to drag the boxes over. One of them tore at the side and she cursed as its contents— photos and papers—spilled out everywhere.

"Shit." She bent to scoop it all up. Fin couldn't help herself— she shuffled through the stack she was holding. In one picture a man stood with his family against the backdrop of the house. She flipped it over and saw *1888* written in faded blue ink. She looked at the man again. Could this be Nathaniel Cushion? There was something familiar about him, but in this light it was hard to see properly.

Fin put the pictures and documents back in the box as best she could and dragged it over to a corner.

Out of curiosity, she opened a few of the other boxes. Most had general junk inside: broken lamps, chipped teacups, and yellowed paperback books. It was the detritus from the families who lived here before. Left down here and forgotten over time. She didn't have time now, but later she might take them upstairs and have a look through. It would be something to occupy her in the evenings while Sadie was away.

It took a few hours, but finally the tunnel was hidden once more, and the basement junk gave no sign she'd struggled through it earlier.

Upstairs again, Fin checked her watch. She'd have enough time for a quick shower and change of clothes before the furniture arrived.

❖

Fin sat on the sofa and put her feet up. The furniture arrived and she'd worked late into the evening, trying to catch up on a piece she was well behind on. All day, she'd thought about the journal and looked forward to reading it. The box still sat in the basement, and Fin wondered what other treasures were in there.

Fin drank from her wine glass and opened the journal at the first entry. It took her a moment to adjust to the handwriting, and she was struck by how beautiful the cursive script was. She felt a sense of loss that no one wrote like that any more.

Unfortunately, the excitement she'd felt all day didn't match what was inside. The first entry concerned itself with practical matters about the house construction. She flicked through several more pages which were filled with the same subject. She skim-read through about a month's worth of entries and almost put the journal down. Finally, she came to a vaguely interesting entry and read:

11th August 1888

I have today been forced to let another of the builders go. I told the man I found his work to be substandard and almost laughed at the shock on his face. He is the fifth man this month. He begged me to reconsider and even came close to tears when he told me about his sick child. I struggled not to laugh at the pathetic creature.

The truth, of course, is far from the story I told him about his shoddy workmanship. I cannot tell him why I fired him or the four before him. I would find myself on the gallows with a noose around my neck if the truth were ever known.

I am impatient. The high turnover of workmen slows the building and I am anxious to take up residence. I have dreamed of this for so long, and now that the wait is almost done, I find myself short of both temper and self-control. I must remain controlled, though. I must, or it will all be for nothing and I am so close.

Fin yawned and closed the journal. Nathaniel Cushion sounded like a bit of a bastard. She was too tired to read any more and decided to call it a night. Perhaps she'd pick it up again tomorrow.

Fin went upstairs to bed. She was asleep almost as soon as her head hit the pillow.

She woke a few hours later gasping for breath. She ran a shaky hand over her head and it came away wet with sweat. It was the dream. That fucking dream.

Fin got out of bed and went into the bathroom. She ran the tap and splashed water over her face. It helped a bit. Except she still couldn't get that dream out of her head. *Fuck.*

In the dream she'd come home to find Lance Sherry at her dining table. By one hand sat a cup of tea, and by the other was a wicked sharp knife. Sadie was at the sink, and when she turned, she had an angry red line across her throat where he'd cut her. In a dreadful monotone voice she'd said, *Welcome home, Fin. We've been waiting for you.* Fin turned at the sound of her children coming through the door, and they had those same red lines too. Fin tried to scream but nothing came out.

See, said Lance Sherry smugly. *This is what happens when you can't take care of your family. I make them mine. Now run along, you pathetic creature.* And he made a shooing motion with his hand. Sadie laughed, except that didn't sound right either.

In the dream, Fin's legs began to move of their own accord and carried her out of the house and down the drive. She turned to look back, and they stood there: Sadie, Sherry, and the kids in the same pose as the photo she found in the basement. Except for those red lines on their throats. The red lines had begun to bleed.

That was when she woke up, terrified. Now she stood in front of the sink, her face and hairline wet. She looked at herself in the mirror. She looked like shit.

Fuck it. Fuck waiting for the police to catch him, and fuck having Sadie and the kids halfway round the world while she sat here twiddling her thumbs. Fin hadn't gotten where she was by waiting for someone else to save her. If she had, she'd still be waiting now. She knew exactly how to put an end to this. Her horrible family would finally be good for something.

She got dressed and went downstairs, grabbing her car keys on the way.

CHAPTER EIGHTEEN

It was almost closing time, but the pub was still packed. The Beggar was one of those pubs the twenty-first century left untouched. It still had two separate bars. In the old days, one had been for working men and the other for men and their wives. Even when she was a kid, her dad would take her to the second bar and usually leave her there with a Coke and a packet of crisps. These days, people used whichever bar they wanted. The carpets were threadbare in places and all the dark wood made the place seem small and dingy. It hadn't changed at all.

Fin's uncles had been drinking in this place for years. Her mum used to send her down to fetch her dad home on Sunday afternoons, back before he walked out and her mum started hitting the bottle.

She was hardly through the door when she heard her name being called.

"Finola? Bloody hell, it's Fin."

"You all right, Nate?" She barely had time to greet her cousin before he pulled her into a bear hug.

He lifted her off her feet and spun her around. "Joe," he called to the barman. "Get my cousin Fin a drink. What do you fancy, Fin?"

"I'll have a vodka Red Bull." She usually didn't touch the stuff, but she was running low on sleep and needed something to lift the fog.

Before long, she was sitting at a table in the corner, wedged between the wall and Nate. Fin looked up to find her Uncle Finlay watching her. Her namesake always reminded her of a lizard. He took in everything around him without ever moving his head. She would bet money he even had a forked tongue.

"How are you, sweetheart?" he asked. "Haven't seen you for years. How's your mum?"

The last time Fin saw her mum, she was in the park drinking cider. Fin had walked past and pretended not to see her. "She's all right. I haven't seen her for a while."

Uncle Finlay nodded. "Heard there was a bit of trouble with your…with Sadie? Isn't it?"

He was quick. She had to give him that. She wasn't surprised he knew about the attack. He'd probably been wondering if she might pop by. He would help, she knew. But it would cost her. Not money, by all accounts he had plenty of that. Uncle Finlay traded in favours. If she took his help, she'd be paying him back forever.

"That was a terrible business. We were all very sorry to hear about it. Is she all right?" he asked. The sympathy in his voice never reached his eyes.

"Thanks, Uncle Finlay. She's okay, yeah."

"Have they caught the little cunt yet?"

He would know they hadn't.

"No."

"Terrible business." He reached forward and picked up his drink, his eyes never leaving hers. He was waiting for her to ask him. She thought about the promise she made Sadie, about the reasons she hadn't spoken to her family for years.

"Do you know him? Lance Sherry?" she asked.

Nate shifted on his seat beside her, and she saw him make eye contact with his dad. "We know of him. He's off the Charles Hocking estate, so we don't tend to, er, cross paths much."

Fin heard what he wasn't saying. Sherry worked for a different firm, which would make things trickier.

"Do you know where he is?" she asked again.

Nate shrugged. "Lying low probably. He's got a few friends left in the area. I can ask around if you want?"

Fin looked around at the pub. It was a relic, just like the men in front of her. Just like most of the people in here. A snapshot of a world that didn't exist any more. Her uncle was still dangerous and he still had connections, but the world was changing and he was a dinosaur. Still dreaming about a world that had long since passed. He was even wearing a fucking suit, for God's sake. To the pub. To this shithole.

What was she doing here? Was she mad? She'd gotten away from these people, and now she was thinking of inviting them back into her life. Into Sadie's life. Into her kids'. This was madness.

"Maybe. How's Aunt Mary?" she asked instead.

Surprise registered in Uncle Finlay's eyes before they hardened and flattened again. "She's good, thanks. Spending most of her time with Michelle now she's had the baby."

Fin vaguely remembered her mum telling that her cousin Michelle had a new baby. "Congratulations," Fin said.

Uncle Finlay waved her off. "She's like a fucking cat, that one. Popping them out all over the place. I should put a cardboard box under the stairs for her and have done with it. You've got kids, haven't you?"

Fin didn't want to talk about her kids. Not with them and not in here. Now all she wanted was to get out and go to bed. Christ knew what she'd been thinking, coming here in the first place. She must be mad.

"Look, Uncle Finlay—"

"No, you look, sweetheart. I haven't got time for games. You want something, else you wouldn't be here, and I think we both know what it is." He spoke quietly and Fin was surprised at his directness.

"It was a mistake to come."

Uncle Finlay made a seesawing motion with his hand. "Depends on how you look at it. I've got business, so you'll need to excuse me. Why don't you stay for a bit and catch up with Nate? You always were his favourite cousin."

She nodded.

He stood up and leaned towards her. "If you come around again, though, Finola, you'd better be sure about what you're after because once a deal's done, it's done. Catch my drift?"

She nodded again. Next time she came here he'd take it as a green light she wanted Sherry killed, and then she'd be his forever.

She stayed for another drink, then made her excuses and left. She was glad to get out of there. The drinks were doubles and she couldn't drive on them. She hailed a cab and headed into the centre of town. She didn't want to go home yet. She felt disconnected and unlike herself.

Fin couldn't believe she'd gone there, to see him. She knew what would have happened. Lance Sherry would be found floating in the river or dumped in a park, and it would have been on her. And the blood would be on her hands. She'd have to face Sadie, knowing what she'd done after she promised not to.

What was so wrong with her that she'd considered ordering a man killed? Even someone like Lance Sherry. Fin had worked so hard to leave these people behind. She had fought not to end up like her cousin Michelle, popping out baby after baby by an endless stream of useless blokes. Used up and exhausted by twenty-eight.

In one night she had almost undone all that hard work. She almost brought those people back into her life. Into Sadie's and her kids' lives.

Fin directed the cabbie to a women's bar in Soho. She needed a drink or ten.

❖

19th September 1893

She still bangs her fists against the door, but there isn't much force behind them any more and it comes much more infrequently. I like to sit on the other side with my ear pressed against it so I can hear her weep and beg me to release her. I am growing bored with Anna, and my wife will return from her mother's home in just a few more days. It wouldn't do for her to find out about my game. Like before, I shall tell her another maid resigned her post while she was away. Sometimes I watch my wife and wonder. I watch her and imagine she was locked behind this door, banging against it in vain. Would it feel different than having Anna in there? Would I enjoy it more? These are questions for another day. Anna has stopped weeping. I'll turn on the gas soon.

Fin woke up and felt sick. It felt like someone was tightening a steel band around her head. She groaned. Something moved beside her and she turned her face to see the top of a woman's head poking out of the duvet.

Her stomach roiled. Oh no, what had she done? She didn't remember much about last night except that she'd started out in a women's bar in town. She had a vague recollection of being in a club and dancing. There had been a woman grinding up against her. What had she done?

Fin sat up and the world tilted on its axis. She thought she might be sick, and she wasn't sure if it was because of the booze or the woman lying next to her.

That was when she noticed she still had her clothes on. *What?* She glanced around and the room seemed familiar too. Fin reached out and pulled the duvet off the sleeping woman next to her.

"Hey! Get lost, Fin."

Fin felt relief wash over her at the sight of her very hungover and very sleepy best friend. She grinned. "Morning. You look rough, Rose."

"Back at you, dickhead."

Fin laughed. "What happened last night?"

"You called me, pissed out of your head. You were all, *Rose come down to the bar, me and Sarah are doing shots.*"

"Sarah?"

"Don't worry, you didn't do anything. You were out of your tiny mind. I tried to bring you home, but you insisted we go clubbing."

"Shit, sorry."

Rose waved off the apology then yawned. "Can you at least make coffee? I feel as rough as a badger's arse."

Fin got up and waited for the room to settle down. Gingerly, she made her way into the bathroom and turned on the shower. She found a couple of aspirin in Rose's cabinet and swallowed them.

In the shower she sniffed Rose's shampoo and decided she'd rather smell of patchouli than beer and cigarettes. She was just starting to feel human when Rose burst in.

"Fin, it's the police. On your phone. I picked it up—"

Fin jumped out of the shower and ran back into the studio room. She felt sick but it wasn't anything to do with the booze.

CHAPTER NINETEEN

Fin put down the phone and turned to face Rose. "They got him," she whispered.

Rose's face turned to pure joy and she pumped her fist. "Yes!"

Fin laughed and pulled her into a hug. She picked her up and swung her around.

Rose squealed. "Umm, Fin."

"What?" Fin grinned.

She lowered Rose to the floor but kept her arms around her.

"Well, as happy as I am for you and Sadie, you might want to put some clothes on."

Fin looked down and realized she was naked. She hadn't thought about it as she'd barrelled out of the shower. "Oops. Sorry."

Rose made a show of looking her up and down, then cocked an eyebrow. "No need to apologize. It's been years since I've seen you naked, and I have to say, you look all right for an old bird."

"I'm thirty-five," Fin muttered. Her face was on fire and she slunk back into the bathroom and shut the door on the sound of Rose's laughter.

Five minutes later and she was dressed. She was wearing the clothes from last night and they stank of stale beer and cigarettes, but at least she felt cleaner. The headache and queasiness were gone. Rose had made coffee and was sitting on the couch with the duvet wrapped around her.

"When did they get him?" she asked.

"Yesterday, late afternoon. They've arrested him for a load of stuff, and he's been denied bail. Which means he's going to be locked up until the trial." They'd picked him up on the south coast, where he'd been staying for the past few days. That meant it would have been difficult for him to have been the one who shut the trapdoor on her.

"That's great news. Does Sadie know?"

"Yeah, they called her first thing. I need to phone her now."

Before she could, the phone rang. It was Sadie.

Fin picked up her mug of coffee and perched on the edge of the sofa. "Hello, babe," she said.

"Did you hear?"

"Yeah, they just called. It's great news."

"It is, it is! I can't believe it. I feel like a weight has been lifted. I managed to get us on a flight that leaves in a few hours. We'll be home tonight."

Fin's heart soared and tears prickled the back of her eyes. She pinched the bridge of her nose to ward them off. "I'm so happy. I've missed you."

"I've missed you. We all have. I'll see you soon. I love you."

"See you soon. I love you too."

Fin hung up and she felt Rose rubbing small circles on her back.

"Aren't you glad you didn't ask your uncle for help now?" Rose asked, startling Fin. "You told me last night."

"Sadie can't ever know about that."

Rose nodded her head. "I won't tell her. But, Fin, if you ever get it into your head to do something stupid like that again—"

"I won't."

"If you *do*. Please call me or something."

Fin nodded. "I will. I promise."

❖

Lance Sherry lay on his bed in his cell. He could almost see the Man perched on the end watching him. He wasn't there. *He wasn't.* But all the same…

"Don't look at me like that. It wasn't my bloody fault," Lance said petulantly. "There's CCTV everywhere in this country. They were bound to catch up with me sooner or later."

A member of the public had recognized him in the chicken shop and called the police. As soon as he stepped outside with his family bucket, he'd been dragged to the ground and handcuffed.

"It's your fault anyway. I wanted to go back to the bitch's house straight away, but you said no, we had to wait."

The Man regarded him silently and Lance felt his anger bubble over. "Fuck you, you don't even speak! How do I know what you want when you don't even fucking speak!"

The flap in the metal door of his cell flicked down and Lance saw two eyes peek through. "Pipe down, Lance. Who are you talking to anyway?"

Lance gave him the finger and turned back to the Man. He carried on in a whisper. "You do realize this is crazy, don't you? That *I'm* crazy. You don't even exist. Christ, I'm losing my mind."

Lance got up and began to pace the small room. He was talking to a figment of his imagination. Seeing something that wasn't there. He didn't feel like he was mad, but he must be… Mustn't he?

Lance turned around to face the Man. The Man smiled and beckoned him over. He had a plan to get out of this place. Lance grinned. He was a man with a plan.

It was after midnight when Sadie and the kids pulled up in front of the house. Fin had wanted to come and collect them from the airport, but the flight was delayed, and Sadie told her it was easier to just take a taxi.

Fin must have been waiting at the window though, because she was out of the front door and at the car door before Sadie had even undone her seat belt.

They carried the children inside. Both of them had fallen asleep on the journey over here. Back in their own bedroom, Sadie drew the curtains. She had switched on the bedside lights leaving the room in a warm glow.

The bedsprings squeaked as Fin got in. Sadie quickly shed her clothes and joined her. Fin lay on her back with her eyes closed. Even in this light Sadie could see the dark circles under her eyes. She traced them with one finger. "Did you get any sleep while we were away?" she asked softly.

Fin's blue eyes opened and caught hers. She smiled. "I went out with Rose last night. It was a late one."

"You went to London?"

"It's empty here without you," Fin replied simply.

Sadie stroked her face. She loved the feel of her soft skin. She traced the arch of her cheekbones and the gentle bow of her lips. "We're back now. We can move forward."

Fin reached up and took her hand. She kissed Sadie's palm and held it against her face. "There's still the trial," she said quietly.

That was true. As a lawyer, Sadie knew how these things went, and it wouldn't be pleasant. She was confident he'd be convicted though—there was too much evidence against him. "I'm not worried about that. He's caught, and the trial is a long way off yet. If he has a good solicitor this time, I imagine he'll be advised to plead guilty."

"So they'll give him a lighter sentence?"

"It'll still be a long one. He tried to kill me. He stalked me after the fact. Don't worry, Fin."

"I'll try not to."

"I don't want to talk about Lance Sherry any more." Sadie slid down so she was pressed against Fin's side.

"Oh? What do you want to talk about then?"

"I don't want to talk at all."

Fin sat up and gasped in mock surprise. "You're trying to seduce me!"

Sadie laughed and pulled Fin down on top of her. She ran her hands up Fin's sides and kissed her.

She felt Fin's thigh push between her legs and against her centre, and the sensation made her moan. She rocked against it, creating the friction she needed to get off. Fin darted away from her, and Sadie almost groaned until she saw where she was going.

Sadie lifted her hips and parted her legs wide as Fin came to rest between them. Fin licked her gently at first, tasting. She began to stroke with her tongue, becoming firmer and more localized on her clit—the way she liked it. When Fin pushed two fingers inside her, Sadie orgasmed. She held on to Fin's head, pulled it against her, urging her to carry on. The second orgasm crashed through her, and she pushed down hard on Fin's fingers.

Fin gentled the strokes with her tongue until she stopped altogether. Sadie felt her plant a soft kiss on her inner thigh, and she reached down to stroke her hair.

She closed her eyes and drifted off to sleep.

CHAPTER TWENTY

When Sadie woke up, Fin was already gone. She reached over and felt Fin's side of the bed. Cold. Sadie was aware of her tossing and turning in the night, and a few times she'd cried out in her sleep. Sadie guessed it was the stress of the last few months, and she was worried about her. Fin had been a rock for her, never complaining and taking on most of the load, much more than she could reasonably be expected to. But she had done it willingly, and Sadie knew she was lucky to have her.

Perhaps it was being away and not seeing her for a few days, but Sadie thought she looked drawn and like she'd lost weight. She seemed exhausted. Sadie decided it was her turn to pick up some of the slack and let Fin rest. She was going to deal with the children this morning but Fin was already up.

Sadie dressed and went into the kitchen. Fin was hunched over the table with Lucy and Liam. They were doing the spot-the-difference puzzle in one of Liam's magazines.

"What time did you get up?" she asked, bending to kiss Fin and brush her hair out of her eyes.

"Miss Lucy decided to get me up at six."

Sadie poured herself coffee. "I could have gotten up with her."

"It's fine—you've been on your own with them. It's probably my turn. Besides, I was already awake."

"Mama." Lucy drew Fin's attention away before Sadie could ask about her bad dreams.

She stood and watched them for a minute. Liam was serious, studying each picture with intent. Lucy tried to turn the page, already bored with the game, while Fin absently batted her hand away then tickled her. Sadie felt a huge swell of love for them. If Lance Sherry'd had his way, they wouldn't be here like this now, and she was again struck by how fragile life was.

Upstairs, a door slammed. Sadie jumped, nearly dropping her mug.

"What was that?" asked Liam, looking worried.

"Koosh," Lucy replied with authority. "He wants to play monster."

❖

Fin had skulked off to the basement while Sadie put the finishing touches on dinner. Rachel would be here soon, and Sadie was looking forward to seeing her. As soon as she'd heard she was back with the children, she'd wanted to come straight down. Sadie offered to put her off, but Fin insisted it would be good for her to have a friend over. Fin bought pizza for herself, Liam, and Lucy, and they planned to have a Pixar night in the back lounge. All that space was one good thing about having this house, Sadie thought.

It wasn't that she didn't like the house, not exactly, but she didn't feel comfortable here either. She supposed it might have something to do with all that had gone on, and she was hoping it would grow on her. There was still time. As well as that, though, she missed London. There wasn't much in the way of local entertainment, and she missed being able to go to the cinema or theatre without planning it first.

She would *try* and like it here, though. She owed Fin that. Fin and Lucy loved the house—Liam, she wasn't sure about. He didn't ever really show his feelings, but Sadie got the distinct impression he felt the same as her. She uncorked the wine just as the doorbell rang.

"It's a great house," Rachel said as they sat at the kitchen table after dinner, drinking wine.

"You like it?"

"I didn't say that. It's perfect for someone like Fin. I just don't see you here."

"What do you mean?"

"It's so...*country*." Rachel waved her glass over her head, sloshing the wine around. She was drunk. "You've always been a city girl."

Sadie made a mental note to make up the bed in the spare room for Rachel. "It's less than half an hour to London."

"To Stratford."

"That's London."

Rachel made a seesawing motion with her free hand. "I mean, what exactly are you going to do out here, anyway? Raise chickens? Go to jumble sales?"

"Maybe I will. Maybe I'll become a fifties style housewife."

"The villagers will be out with their pitchforks for you. Are there any other same-sex biracial families here?"

"Rachel, you're making it sound like *The Wicker Man*. We're half an hour from London—most of the people here are Londoners who've moved out. You know, I even saw another black person today in the town. There wasn't a pitchfork in sight. You're so bloody dramatic."

"I'm just saying, moving somewhere like this. Fin wouldn't even think about it but—"

"Rachel. Enough."

Rachel held up her hands in surrender. "Okay, sorry. You love it here, Fin's going to start baking, and you'll pop out more babies. I get it."

Sadie laughed. "I don't know about more babies. I think we're happy with the two we've got. Anyway, what about you? Any prospects on the horizon?"

Rachel shook her head. "I'm shagging a paediatrician. Probably the closest I'll get to children."

"She's not a long-term possibility?"

"No. She's great and she has magic fingers but—"

"Sorry, sorry," Fin interrupted, pushing open the door. "We need more juice."

"If they wet the bed you're cleaning it up," Sadie said.

"Finola Claiborne. How are you?" Rachel was beginning to slur her words. "Don't I get a kiss?"

Fin leaned down and pecked her on the cheek from behind. To Sadie, she did a driving mime followed by a drinking one and raised her eyebrow in question.

"Rachel's staying with us tonight."

"Like hell I am," she said.

"You aren't driving."

"I'll get a cab."

"It'll cost a fortune."

"I have a considerable disposable income," she shot back and Fin laughed.

"If she doesn't want to stay, babe, let her call a cab."

Fin poured out two glasses of juice, then watered them down. "Okay, have fun, ladies."

And then she was gone.

"Why won't you stay?" Sadie asked.

Rachel huffed. "Fine. I'll stay. Happy now?"

"Yes."

They opened another bottle of wine, and Sadie knew she'd regret it in the morning, but she was having such a nice time.

"So, tell me." Rachel leaned across the table on her elbows which nearly slipped. "Are you serious about staying here? Because I'm hearing rumours out of your old chambers."

Sadie sipped her wine and pursed her lips. "What rumours?"

"They're going to offer you your old job back, with a raise."

Sadie didn't know what to say. Part of her was thrilled, and the other part didn't want anything to do with it. "How do you know this?"

Rachel shrugged. "A little bird I'm fucking told me."

"The paediatrician?" Sadie was confused.

Rachel waved her hand dismissively. "No, not her. Philippa Monaghan."

"She's into women?" Sadie hadn't known that about her. Then, why would she?

"I think you're focusing on the wrong part of the story," Rachel said.

"I'm not going back there. I can't."

Sadie remembered that night, stepping out of the door, feeling someone come up fast behind her, and then—

Rachel reached across and held her hand. "Shit, I'm sorry. I shouldn't have brought it up. Are you okay? Are you going to have a panic attack?"

"Give me a second," Sadie managed to get out. She forced herself to take measured deep breaths. After a moment, she felt better. She had a healthy swallow of wine. "I'm okay now."

"Good. I really am sorry—"

Sadie held up her hand. "It's not your fault. I have been thinking about going back to work, a lot actually. But it won't be there and probably a different field altogether. I'm thinking about practicing family law."

"Why?" Rachel asked, stunned.

Sadie grinned. "I think it has something to do with the attack. I feel like I want to help people."

"You do. You get them out of prison sentences."

"People who deserve it. People who can't afford the kind of legal assistance we provide. I know what it's like to be a victim, to feel helpless."

Rachel studied her for a moment. She was drunk, but her eyes were still sharp. She had always been able to read Sadie like a book. "Okay, I think I understand. I suppose someone has to help the great unwashed."

Sadie laughed and threw the cork at her friend. "Such a snob."

❖

Sadie and Rachel had moved into the front reception to carry on drinking. Fin stayed where she was. The kids had fallen asleep in front of the TV, and she was content to leave them there amongst their duvets and cushions.

She picked up Nathaniel Cushion's diary and opened it to where she'd left it last. She had to admit, it was pretty dry and mostly talked about the building of the house. She flicked through, noting that Cushion got through quite a few more builders before the work was completed and never explained why, though he hinted that he didn't want anyone knowing about the exact layout, which seemed odd to Fin.

She was about to put it back down, bored, when she found an entry that made her blood run cold. He talked about wanting to hire a maid:

She should not be from the area or have much in the way of family and friends. No one must miss her.

Fin skipped through several more pages until she came to another journal entry.

She screams so loudly. I am relieved there are no neighbours nearby. Last night she screamed for almost half an hour without stopping. In the end I was forced to turn on the gas.

What the fuck was this? Some kind of joke? It must be a windup, Fin thought. She picked up her phone and brought up the internet. She typed in *Nathaniel Cushion* and got a couple of hits.

Fin clicked on the first link, and the first thing she saw was a grainy photograph. The man staring back at her could have been Uncle Finlay. Her hand shook and saliva filled her mouth. Fin thought she might be sick.

She forced herself to read the article beneath. One of the kids groaned from under the duvet but she barely registered it.

According to the article, Nathaniel Cushion had been a con man. He was involved in a bit of bodysnatching—not uncommon for the time—and insurance fraud. He'd been arrested and hanged in 1937 when one of his scams caught up with him. The article said one of his associates went missing in unusual circumstances and later turned up dead. Cushion had claimed on an insurance policy he took out on the man several months before. At the same time, he'd sold a cadaver to a London surgeon, that turned out to be the same associate.

When police went to his house, they found evidence he had used the basement to prepare cadavers for sale to doctors. They suspected he might have killed others for insurance money but found no evidence to confirm it. They also couldn't find any evidence to prove he murdered his wife and two of his children. Cushion told friends and neighbours they sailed to America the previous year, though no sign of them was found on any ship manifest or at customs in New York. Cushion was survived by one adult son, Finlay. It was believed Finlay changed his name after the scandal.

The second link contained much of the same information, only expanding slightly on the theory that Nathaniel Cushion was a serial killer. Once he was arrested, Cushion never spoke again despite numerous attempts by newspapers and the police to interview him.

This was his house then. Fin looked around at the beautiful detail in the cornicing and the ornate fireplace. How could someone like that design such a lovely home? Or was it just her who thought it was lovely? Sadie didn't like it. Liam didn't like it either. Perhaps she'd been drawn here because this monster was a relative? She dismissed the thought immediately as stupid. It was coincidence there was family resemblance to Cushion. And the recurrence of names...well, that must be coincidence too. It was impossible she was related to him and living in his house.

Wasn't it? *Yes.* Even if it was true, what difference did it make? Nathaniel Cushion was long dead and wouldn't be bothering them. She couldn't go back to Uncle Finlay and ask about it because she was lucky to get away from him the last time without signing her soul away.

One thing she was certain of: Sadie mustn't know. She felt strongly—instinctively—that Sadie must never know about Nathaniel Cushion and his connection with their house. For the first time, Sadie was actually spending time at home and allowing Fin to concentrate on her business without having to worry about who would pick the kids up if she took on that extra job. Fin was enjoying being able to focus on her own needs for once, and if Sadie got a whiff of something creepy going on, she'd up sticks and move them back to London. She'd go straight back to work as a barrister, and everything would go back the way it was.

Fin picked up the journal and put it on the bookcase, making sure to hide it amongst a couple of other books so it would be inconspicuous. Satisfied, she switched off the lights and went to bed.

CHAPTER TWENTY-ONE

As Rachel told her she would, Sadie got a phone call from her old chambers a few days later offering her old job back. She declined.

"We're okay for money for a while longer," Fin told her. The weather was cool and they'd lit a fire in the wood burner. The children were tucked up in bed, and the evening stretched out in front of them. Sadie supposed now was as good a time as any to tell Fin about her plans.

"I am ready to go back to work," she said, swirling the red wine around her glass. Fin lay with her head in Sadie's lap and opened her eyes to look up.

"What, now?"

"Well, not this minute, but yes. I started looking today." She sifted Fin's blond strands though her fingers. She loved Fin's hair. "I registered with a recruitment agency."

Fin sat up and reached for her wine on the coffee table. "Right. Thanks for checking it with me first."

Sadie worked to hold on to her temper. "I wasn't aware I needed your permission."

"Don't do that." Fin turned to look at her. She seemed angry. "You know what I meant. Sorry I don't have the wide and varied vocabulary you do. I meant you didn't discuss it with me."

"You always knew I wanted to go back to work. What would we have discussed?"

"Whether it was the right time? Lance Sherry hasn't even gone to trial yet. And things have been so up in the air. I'm getting more customers, so we aren't strapped for money."

"You're worried about me, then? Is that why you don't want me to go back to work?"

Fin shrugged, drank more wine. "I just don't know why you're in such a rush."

"I've been off for nearly six months. I'm going stir crazy. I love the children but—"

"But you want to go back the way things were. My job coming second. Me picking them up from school, me putting them to bed, while you work sixty hour weeks again. Yeah, that sounds great."

"Why are you being so argumentative?"

Fin didn't answer her. Instead she got up and put more wood on the fire even though it didn't need it. Sadie was confused by the whole conversation. Fin had always been supportive of her career, and vice versa. She had been acting differently the last few days. She wasn't sleeping well and was up before even Lucy. She looked tired and was losing weight.

Sadie went over to where she still stood, staring into the fire. She snaked her arms around Fin from behind and kissed her neck. "I'm sorry if you feel like I ambushed you. I honestly thought you knew I wanted to go back to work. We can talk about it if you like. About your reservations."

Fin sighed and Sadie felt her body relax. "No, you're right. I'm being an arsehole. Of course you should go back to work. I just…"

"What?" Sadie asked softly.

"I don't know. It doesn't matter." Fin pulled out of the embrace and went back to the sofa. "I'm just tired. Let's watch a film or something." She picked up the remote and turned on the television.

Typical Fin. She always shut down like this. Sometimes, Sadie could push and coax it out of her. She sensed now wasn't that time.

She sat down next to Fin and poured them more wine, studied her wife's profile in the light of the television. Fin's jaw was tensed, her lips pressed in a tight line. Something was bothering her. Sadie wanted to talk about why she felt like her career was sidelined. She had never meant to make her feel that way. It would have to wait until Fin was in a more relaxed state, because she wasn't in the mood to discuss anything, and they'd end up rowing instead. She tried to concentrate on the film.

❖

Fin sat up. She was soaked with sweat and it was hard to breathe. Sadie was asleep beside her and Fin was relieved. These dreams were getting worse. Every night now, she dreamed Lance Sherry was in her kitchen, and every night she walked away from the house to see her family posing with him like the photo in the basement. What the fuck was going on? It didn't make any sense at all.

As she lay back down, she heard a scream. Liam.

Fin threw off the covers and raced down the stairs and along the hall to his room. He was sitting up in bed and soaked in sweat, just as she'd been a few moments ago.

Fin sat down beside him and pulled him into her arms. "You're dreaming, Liam. It's just a dream. Wake up now." She shook him gently and his eyes popped open. Fin sensed Sadie in the doorway. "Liam? Liam can you see me?" He continued to stare vacantly at her.

Fin turned to talk to Sadie, but she wasn't there. Instead, it was Nathaniel Cushion, and he was dressed in a dirty white coat—like a doctor. He held a scalpel.

Fin looked back to Liam, and that was when she realized it wasn't sweat he was soaked in. It was blood. He was dead. The man had already been in here. *Lucy.* Fin laid Liam back onto the sheets and turned. Cushion was closer now. He looked down at her and smiled. He shook his head and placed one finger over his lips. He held the knife above his head and Fin knew he meant to kill her too. She didn't care, though. Liam was dead and she didn't care.

Fin gasped and came awake. She sat bolt upright and dragged a shaking hand through her hair. It was dripping wet. *Liam.*

She threw off the covers and hurried out of the room.

Liam was in his bed and very much alive. She felt relief wash over her. She put her hand on his chest and was comforted by the steady rise and fall.

Fin watched him for a while. He opened his eyes and found hers. He had that faraway look which told her he was still asleep, but when he spoke he sounded very much awake.

"You don't have to kill us," he muttered. His eyes closed, and he rolled onto his side.

Fin was dumfounded. It was on the tip of her tongue to say, *It isn't me, it's him that kills you.* She didn't know where that thought came from—it sounded so alien in her head. And the thought placed the action in the future. As if it was something she was going to do.

She just needed a proper night's sleep, that was all. If she could just get to sleep, she knew she would feel better. One night without those dreams. Fin stood and wearily headed back to bed.

CHAPTER TWENTY-TWO

Fin buttered her toast and took a bite. Out of the corner of her eye she could see Sadie watching her. After her dream last night, she hadn't been able to go back to sleep. She'd been in the workshop since four. She guessed that was the plus side—she was ahead of schedule with work.

Fin yawned and realized Lucy was talking to her. "Sorry, sweetheart, what was that?"

"Koosh wants you to play with us."

"Koosh? Oh, that's your imag—" Sadie kicked her under the table. "Your friend."

Lucy nodded and swallowed another mouthful of cereal. "He woked me up last night. You won't hurt us, will you, Mama?"

Fin dropped her toast. She was aware Liam was watching her with interest, as if the same question was in his head. She looked between the two of them.

"Of course Mama wouldn't ever hurt either of you," Sadie spoke up.

"Luce, who is this Koosh?" Fin asked.

"He's bad," Liam said.

"No, he's not. He's my friend," Lucy said.

"He's not even real."

"Liam. Enough," Sadie said.

Fin looked at her son and shivered, remembering her nightmare.

She quickly gulped down her coffee and stood. "I need to get to work."

She felt Sadie's eyes boring into her. "Do you have to go now? You look so tired."

"I'm fine." She grabbed a piece of toast.

"Maybe you could come back for a nap after lunch?"

"Nope. Too busy. That kid from town is coming up today."

She sensed Sadie was about to say something else, when there was a knock at the kitchen door. Saved by the bell.

Fin pulled it open and Floyd Dodson was standing there. He was eighteen, six feet two, and built like a string bean. He was pretty in that way some boys were before they fully reached maturity. He reminded her of Liam. Floyd looked innocent and struck her as a bit vulnerable. But he was strong and, from what she'd seen the other day, a hard worker too.

"Morning, Floyd."

"Hello, Mrs. Claiborne."

"I told you, call me Fin." She moved away from the door and gestured to her family inside. "That's my wife, Sadie, and those are our kids, Liam and Lucy. Kids, say hello to Floyd."

"Hello, Floyd," they said in unison.

"Do you want to get a cup of tea or coffee before we go?"

He shook his head. "No, thanks. I don't like hot drinks."

Sadie stood and came to the door. "We've got juice. Do you want to come in?"

Floyd hopped from one foot to the other, his brow furrowed. "No, thank you. I don't want to come in."

Fin raised her eyebrows at Sadie. "Let's go then." She took her jacket off the hook and stepped outside. Sadie touched her shoulder.

"Lunch is at twelve. Floyd, do you like pasta?"

Floyd scrunched his brow again and held up a clear plastic lunchbox. "My mum made my lunch already." His eyes landed on something behind them, in the house. He gulped and his eyes bugged out. Fin turned but only saw the kids eating their breakfast. For some reason, her thoughts went to Nathaniel Cushion. She didn't know why.

"Let's go, Floyd," she said.

As she closed the kitchen door, she heard Lucy say, "Koosh is here," in an excited voice.

They walked in companionable silence down to the workshop.

"Can I trust you with a secret?" Fin asked Floyd.

"I think so. Yes," Floyd answered.

"I've got a surprise for the kids. It's a playset and I need help putting it up."

Floyd's eyes lit up with childish enthusiasm. "I'd love to help. Where is it?" He looked around the workshop.

"It's in the van." She nodded to a Luton van parked out front. "Sadie's taking them into town, so we'll put it up once they've gone."

Floyd nodded and grinned. Fin returned it. He had one of those smiles that made you want to smile too.

Fin was feeling better than she had in days. She was still exhausted—still haunted by those awful dreams—but the idea of doing something nice for the kids made her happy. She supposed it had something to do with realizing one of her own childhood fantasies. A big wooden playset on a big lawn outside a big house.

They soon got to work, stripping an antique armchair that probably cost as much as all her own furniture did new. She kept an eye out for Sadie leaving with the kids.

❖

Fin squinted at the instructions and turned them upside down to see if they made more sense that way. Shit, it was like trying to read hieroglyphics. "Floyd. Can you make this out?" she asked.

Floyd ambled over and took the instructions off her. "Yes." He barely glanced at them before handing them back.

Floyd turned out to be an instruction manual reading genius, and she was happy to follow his orders as the playset went up with ease.

When they finished, Fin fetched them a glass of water each, and they sat at the picnic bench. "Thanks so much for that, Floyd. I don't think I could have done it without you."

Floyd shrugged. "You're welcome, Mrs. Claiborne."

"I've told you before, call me Fin."

He looked uncertain but nodded.

"How long have you lived around here, Floyd?"

"All my life."

"You like it?" she asked.

Floyd shrugged again. "I like it."

"Did you know the people who lived in this house before us?"

Floyd suddenly looked nervous. "I helped them like I help you. My mum looked after their kids."

Fin knew Floyd's mum was a childminder. With Sadie insisting on going back to work, they would probably need her services. Fin pushed down the annoyance. "Why did they move?"

She watched as his gaze slipped away from hers and focused somewhere behind her. "They didn't like the house," he said.

"I thought a family member got sick back in France."

Floyd shook his head. "They didn't like the house. The kids didn't like the house. They used to cry when it was time to go home."

"Why didn't they like the house?" Fin asked, not really sure if she wanted an answer.

Floyd hesitated. "It's a bad house. That's what they said, and I agree with them. The little boy got very sick, and so they left."

"Sick how?"

"My mum said he had fits. He had nightmares too. The ambulance came one night and the family never came back."

Fin was silent. This was the last thing she needed Sadie hearing about. Why did everyone think this place was bad? And what did it say about her that she didn't?

"Look, Floyd, let's keep this to ourselves for now, okay?"
Floyd nodded.

"Good. Time to get back to work."

Floyd stood and Fin thought he seemed relieved to be moving out of the shadow of the house.

❖

Fin stood and watched her kids, with an arm around Sadie and a stupid grin on her face. Lucy had bolted out of the car, squealed, and run straight to the newly erected playset, climbing up the ladder and running around like a lunatic. Liam was excited too, but as was his nature, he was much more reserved with his investigation. He walked around the outside, trailing one hand over the freshly cut wood. He pulled on the rope swing, tested the netting she'd staked into the ground and attached to an opening on the top of the playset. At Lucy's insistence he finally used the ladder to climb inside.

Sadie tugged on the back of her shirt and she turned to face her. "That was a lovely thing to do, darling."

Fin smiled. "I'm glad they like it."

"I had no idea what you were planning." Sadie tipped her head up and Fin lowered hers to kiss her. One of the kids yelled, "Yuck!" Fin thought it was Lucy.

"If you're good," Fin said to Sadie, "I'll let you play with it later."

"Hmm." She pretended to consider. "There's something else you have I'd much rather play with." She lifted her eyebrows suggestively.

Fin laughed and smacked her arse playfully. "So naughty."

They both looked back again to watch their children play. Floyd was pushing them alternately on the swings. Fin felt light and happy. The cloud which had been over her all week finally lifted, and she could breathe much more easily. It had been a shitty six months, and she could finally see the proverbial sun poking through. Thank God. Maybe the dreams would go as well—it was probably all stress related anyway. Who wouldn't be stressed with all they'd been through?

She decided this weekend she would take Sadie somewhere nice. Out to dinner or the ballet in London. They both loved the ballet. Sadie had dragged her along when they were first going out. She hadn't been looking forward to it at all. It seemed to be something rich people did and, frankly, total bullshit and a waste of money.

Fin had taken her seat fully preparing to hate it. It was the first of many occasions in her relationship with Sadie where she'd been pleasantly surprised. As she'd watched the dancers leap, vault, and spin across the stage, she'd been mesmerized. The sheer physicality and power of the women and men stunned her. From that first time, she was hooked. The next week, Sadie took her to the opera, but she really couldn't get on board with that at all.

Fin bent and kissed Sadie again. "I need to get back to work, babe."

"Okay. I'll call you for lunch." Sadie gave her a quick pinch on her bum and Fin yelped in surprise.

"Let's put the children to bed early tonight." She winked and Fin couldn't help but laugh.

❖

The afternoon was so mild, Sadie decided to serve lunch outside. It meant the children could carry on playing on the playset and she and Fin could watch them—well, watch Lucy, more like. She'd discovered the joy of jumping from the top of the slide to the ground. Sadie's heart leapt into her throat the first time she'd caught her doing it. She was dreading Lucy's teenage years if this was what she was like at three. Lucy didn't have any fear—she never had. She reminded Sadie of her sister. And Sadie had been around for Rena's teenage years too and seen first-hand how that went.

Liam was the complete opposite, and Sadie worried about him just as much, though for different reasons. He found it hard to make friends and was so quiet you could forget he was in the room. He was so self-contained, but he saw everything. He took it all in and seemed so grown-up sometimes, but he was also vulnerable, much more so than Lucy. Maybe because he was small for his age—he took after her and had a slender frame.

He walked towards her now and she smiled. "Hi, darling. How's the playset?" She stroked his head, flattening his soft, curly hair.

"I like it. Do you want to watch me swing by myself?" he asked.

"In a little while I do. We're going to eat first."

"Out here?"

"Yes. Is that okay?"

He nodded enthusiastically. "I don't like it in there."

"What, in the kitchen?" she asked.

"The house," he clarified.

Sadie sat in one of the wooden chairs and pulled him onto her lap. He leaned back into her, and she hugged him tight. "Why don't you like the house? Do you miss your friends?"

He sighed. "No. I told Mum, it's the *house*."

Sadie turned him around on her lap so he was facing her. "When did you tell her you didn't like the house?"

"I don't know. But I don't like it here, Mummy."

"Why not?"

He shrugged and leaned forward into her. Her arms came around him automatically.

Sadie wasn't sure what to do. Of course she wanted her children to live somewhere they were happy, but unless he told her why he didn't like it here, they could hardly just move on the whim of a six-year-old.

Liam hadn't seemed himself lately. She had barely noticed because she'd been so wrapped up in the Lance Sherry business. Sadie felt guilty. She'd put his mood down to all the upheaval but hadn't actually taken the time to ask him what was wrong. He said he'd told Fin too. Maybe he'd told her more than he'd told Sadie? The two of them were especially close. Although, lately…when she thought about it now, their usual bond hadn't seemed as strong. Maybe she was imagining it. It had been an awful six months, and they all needed time to adjust and get back to normal.

Sadie squeezed Liam and kissed his head. "Why don't you go and tell Mum and Floyd lunch is ready?"

He nodded and slid off her lap. Sadie watched him run off towards the workshop. She was struck again by how vulnerable he seemed. She started setting their lunch up on the table when something made her look up. She was just in time to see Lucy about to jump from the top of the slide.

Chapter Twenty-three

Sadie watched her fall as if in slow motion. One minute she was at the top of the slide waving at Fin, Floyd, and Liam as they walked back across the lawn. The next moment it was as if something pushed her from behind and she fell. It was the only way Sadie could describe it. The way Lucy pitched forward—stumbled, almost—made it look as though someone had shoved her hard.

Before she even hit the ground, Sadie was running. The playset wasn't that high and the ground beneath was spongy, but all the same, Sadie ran to her daughter as fast as she could.

She reached her at the same time as Fin, and they dropped to the ground together. Lucy was crying, and when Sadie held out her arms, Lucy threw herself into them, then screamed.

Sadie held her back gently looking her up and down to see what was wrong.

"I think she's broken her arm." Fin saw it first. "Look."

Lucy had a long-sleeved shirt on, but her arm poked at the shirt and kinked in a strange angle at the elbow.

Fin brushed her hand lightly over Lucy's hair. "We need to take her to A & E." Sadie watched her stand and brush the grass from her jeans. Her face had turned to stone, and Sadie knew she would be feeling like this was all her fault.

She sighed and stood with Lucy in her arms, careful to avoid jostling her injured arm. Lucy dropped her head onto Sadie's shoulder, and Sadie rubbed her back in soothing circles.

"I'll watch Liam if you like." Floyd spoke up, concern etched on his young face.

Sadie hesitated—she barely knew this boy—but before she could object, Fin said, "Thanks, Floyd, we appreciate it." Sadie watched Fin bend down to their son. "Be good for Floyd, okay? We shouldn't be too long. Floyd, we'll call Sadie's parents to come, so you shouldn't have him for more than an hour."

"Can I come with you?" Liam looked as though he might burst into tears.

"No, mate. I need you to stay here with Floyd, okay? We need to go now." Sadie smiled as Fin gave Liam a quick hug, squeezed him tight, and ruffled his hair.

❖

Liam watched his parents drive away from the house with his sister. This house was *bad*. He'd been trying to tell them for ages, but they wouldn't listen. The house scared him, and there were things here that wanted to hurt them. Now it had hurt his sister. He'd told her not to play with Koosh. Lucy thought Koosh was fun, but Liam knew better. Koosh wasn't even a kid.

He looked up at Floyd, his mum's friend who worked for her. Floyd looked down at him and smiled. He smiled back because that's what you did when someone smiled at you.

"What do you want to do?" Floyd asked.

Liam shrugged. He didn't want to go back in the house, that was for sure. "I don't want to go inside."

Floyd looked back at the house and took a big gulp like a cartoon character. Liam thought he looked scared. "No, me either. I don't like your house. Let's walk down to the trees."

"Why don't you like our house?" Liam walked alongside him.

"It's bad. I went in once and—" Floyd shut his mouth and quickly looked at Liam. "I shouldn't say."

"Why not?"

"It'll scare you, and then your parents will be mad with me."

"I'm not a baby. Lucy's a baby but I'm six." Liam held up six fingers to prove his point.

"There's a man who lives in there. He's bad. He's always lived in there."

"Koosh," Liam said.

"Huh?" Floyd pulled back some low hanging branches so they wouldn't hit Liam as he walked through.

"That's what Lucy calls him. It's not his proper name, though. My parents can't see him, but he's always there. All the time. Why's he living in our house?"

"Because it's his house really, and he doesn't like anyone else living there. I don't go inside any more. Don't tell anyone, but he scares me." Floyd went red in his face, and Liam patted him, like Mum did when Liam was sad about something.

"Don't worry. I am too."

Floyd's face brightened. "Do you want to see something cool?"

Liam nodded. He was worried about Lucy and the house and Koosh. It would be nice to see something cool.

Lance Sherry sat in his cell listening to the other inmates playing pool and talking shit outside. He'd been denied bail and would have to sit in here on remand for months before his trial. It wasn't prison so much that bothered him. He'd done a couple of stretches before, and it was easy enough. No, it was the thought of that bitch out there, living her life while he was locked up like an animal.

It wasn't right. All she had to do was keep her flapping lips shut and take his money and get him off. She'd decided to take his money and brush him off like he was some worthless piece of shit. All of this was her fault. He needed to get out of here and teach her a fucking lesson. His new lawyer wanted him to plead guilty. Said it was the best chance he had of getting his sentence reduced and being out within a few years if he behaved inside.

The smarmy little shit didn't understand, though. Lance would happily stay in this place for the rest of his life if it meant getting *her*. And he couldn't do it from behind bars. No, he needed to get out, get that bitch, and then who cared what happened after that? If he could, he'd go abroad again, but it didn't really matter. As long as she suffered. As long as she looked into his eyes as she died and understood that Lance Sherry was someone.

Lance was having dreams now too. Dreams where he killed her and her family. Lance wasn't sure about killing kids—even he had his limits—but the Man told him it was the only way he could get what he wanted. Lance did something for the Man, the Man did something for him. The Man had a plan. A good one. Lance was getting impatient, and though he didn't want to admit it, he was scared of the Man. Something about him…Even though he wasn't here, *couldn't* be here, Lance felt his presence all the same. He could see him, sitting motionless on the end of the bed. Day and bloody night. Lance couldn't get the Man out of his head. And he was obsessed with the bitch's woman. Lance wasn't to touch her. Lance wondered, what was so fucking special about her?

Didn't matter, though. As long as he got *her*. Lance briefly wondered if he was losing his mind, but then he shook the thought off like a bothersome fly.

Chapter Twenty-four

F in threw a piece of wood into the centre of the basement. She told Sadie she was coming down here to tidy up, but the truth was she couldn't look at Lucy with her bright purple cast without feeling guilty.

What was she thinking, buying that playset? Sadie said it was one of those things—even Treven Tate didn't hold it against her. Kids fell off things and broke bones all the time. So why did she feel so guilty about it? At the hospital, they'd asked a lot of questions, and Fin felt like a criminal under the doctor's scrutiny. They had a job to do, she knew that, but their questions made her feel like a child beater, all the same. Lucy's name was probably flagged on a list somewhere now.

Thank God, Sadie hadn't told the doctor about something pushing Lucy off the playset. That probably would have convinced them she and Sadie were bad parents—on drugs or something. Sadie had said it again that night in bed. She told Fin she swore it looked like someone pushed her from behind, the way she jolted forward and stumbled. It was nonsense, but it freaked Sadie out all the same. And now Fin was worried she'd want to move back to her parents'.

She hadn't said anything yet, but it wouldn't be long. Maybe she even made it up as an excuse to leave the house, to leave Fin. She could be fucking selfish sometimes, a spoiled princess. Fin loved her, but her attitude could do with a few adjustments. Fin looked down and noticed she had snapped a bit of wood in half. She needed to get hold of herself. She threw the wood into the pile with the rest.

Fin crouched on the cold basement floor and wiped her sweaty hair out of her eyes. She sighed. She couldn't hide down here forever, but maybe she could get away with it until lunchtime. Sometimes it seemed like she was the only one trying to make this new start work. Liam was moping around with the weight of the world on his shoulders, like he was in prison rather than in a beautiful house surrounded by fields and trees. If he wasn't careful, he was going to end up like his other mother—a spoiled brat. It wasn't entirely his fault, though. Between Sadie and her parents coddling and spoiling him, it was no wonder he was turning out like this. Scared of the dark, and he'd even started wetting the bed again.

Fin's eyes caught on something over at the far wall. She stood and walked over, trailing her hand along the breeze blocks. Breeze blocks. Not very nineteenth century. Someone must have bricked up this part of the basement more recently. Why, though? Fin wondered what was behind there. She picked up the mallet she'd been breaking down some of the furniture with and used it to knock out part of one block.

It crumbled fairly easily and she peeked through. It was pitch dark, but she could make out metal. She squeezed her hand inside to touch it. Cold. Definitely metal. Fin picked up the mallet and began to knock out more blocks.

Sadie splashed hot water onto the worktop at the first sound of banging. What was Fin doing down there? She'd spent the last two days in the basement. Clearing it out, she told Sadie. Sadie knew it was an excuse to stay out of the way. Ever since Lucy's accident she'd become more and more withdrawn. Sadie knew she still wasn't sleeping, and last night she hadn't even come up to bed. Sadie had looked out their bedroom window at three in the morning and seen the light on in the workshop. She was worried about her. Worried about what this house was doing to her.

Fin completely dismissed her when she'd told her about Lucy being pushed off the playset. When Sadie insisted, Fin got angry and accused her of trying to sabotage their new start. Fin had never behaved like that before they moved here. Yes, she had a temper, but she'd never directed it at Sadie. Not that she'd actually done anything to Sadie, hadn't really raised her voice all that much, but the threat was there. Sadie couldn't explain it, but the way Fin looked at her…For a moment Sadie wondered if she might hit her.

Everything was back to normal the next day except that when she noticed Fin's eyes on her, they weren't loving any more. There was a coldness to them that Sadie didn't like. She was starting to look at Liam in the same way.

Another crash came from downstairs, and then it went silent. Sadie was about to call out to Fin to check she was okay, but then she heard her move again—God only knew what she was doing.

Sadie finished making her cup of tea and checked the clock. Almost lunch. Rachel had taken the children out for a while. She was staying the weekend with them and told Sadie she wanted some time alone with her godchildren. Sadie knew she was really just giving Sadie and Fin a break. Rachel had noticed the dark circles under Fin's eyes and the tension between the two of them. No doubt Rachel would question Sadie about it later. She wasn't looking forward to it.

Behind her the kitchen door opened, and she turned to see Fin standing there, a strange look on her face. It took Sadie a moment to realize what it was. It was the look she got when she was horny, except this time there was something different about it, something almost predatory, and Sadie wasn't sure if she liked it or not.

She leaned back against the kitchen counter. "What were you doing down there?"

Fin stepped into the room. There were smudges of dirt on her face and she was sweaty. She moved beside Sadie and washed her hands. "Tidying," was all she said. She looked up from washing her hands and gave Sadie the once over, pausing on her breasts and licking her lips.

Sadie felt the familiar tingle of arousal she always got when Fin looked at her like that—well, not quite in the way she was looking at her now, but something similar.

Fin put down the dishcloth she was drying her hands on and moved into Sadie's personal space. She gripped her hips, fingers digging into Sadie's sides, and Sadie gasped. The tingle became an electric jolt straight to her centre.

"What time is Rachel back with the kids?" Fin's mouth was inches from hers.

"At least another hour," Sadie replied, her centre starting to pulse.

Without warning, Fin kissed her hard. She forced her tongue into Sadie's mouth and kissed her with bruising force. This was new. The Fin Sadie knew was always gentle, no matter how excited she got. But something about this rough, demanding Fin was turning her on too. Her pussy clenched as Fin sucked Sadie's tongue hard into her mouth.

Sadie broke away but kept her lips against Fin's. "Yes, Fin. Yes."

Fin spun her around and bent her over the kitchen table, face down, her hand on the back of Sadie's neck. Something inside her started to tighten as panic rose. Before it could take hold, Fin let go of her neck as if she realized what she was doing, and the panic abated.

Sadie felt Fin fumble with her jeans, heard the zip dragged down as she waited for what Fin would do next.

Fin's hands were on Sadie's backside, kneading and stroking the flesh there. Sadie ground herself against the edge of the table, trying to seek some relief for her pussy which was swollen and wet. Her knickers were soaked through and uncomfortable.

Fin seemed to feel her need, and suddenly, she was pulling Sadie's jeans and knickers down her legs to her ankles. Rough hands parted her cheeks and Sadie groaned as cool air touched her sensitive parts.

"Fuck, you're wet," came Fin's voice from behind her, gravelly and full of need.

The sound of it made Sadie's pussy contract. "Hurry, Fin," she whispered.

Fin slid one finger from Sadie's clit and up to her anus and Sadie moaned. "Your cunt is so fucking wet."

Sadie balked at that. She hated that word and Fin knew it. Before she could protest, Fin's fingers were either side of her clit, stroking roughly, squeezing it firmly, then probing at her entrance. Her other hand gripped Sadie's wrists and held her arms flat on the table above her head. Sadie began to grind into her hand, desperate now for some relief.

"You like that?" Fin asked, leaning over her body and whispering against her ear.

Sadie nodded, trying to push herself on Fin's fingers.

"Say it. Say you like what I'm doing to you. Say you like being bent over this table and getting fucked hard."

Fin's hand stilled and Sadie groaned.

"Say it, or I'll stop."

Fin had never been like this before. Sometimes they'd had hurried sex when the children were smaller. Sometimes they'd had hard, sweaty sex when they'd still been in the early days and couldn't get enough of each other. Whatever kind of sex they had, it was always loving, and Fin was always present. This felt like something else, but Sadie couldn't honestly say she wasn't enjoying it, because she was. There was a hardness to Fin she was usually careful to hide from Sadie. Not today, though. Today Sadie felt her detachment, but Fin's coldness only seemed to make Sadie hotter.

"I like it when you bend me over the table, Fin. I need you to fuck me hard. So stop talking about it and do it."

Sadie cried out as Fin entered her from behind. She felt her own muscles tighten around Fin's fingers, loving the way she pumped in and out of her, her thumb brushing against her clit.

Sadie distantly heard the table squeaking against the floor from the force of Fin fucking her. Sadie felt herself stretch around Fin's fingers, and she cried out when Fin pressed her pussy against Sadie's backside and started humping her.

Sadie focused on the wet sound of Fin's fingers sliding in and out of her, the sound of Fin's moans as she ground against Sadie's arse. Her orgasm began to build, her pussy heavy and pulsing with it. Fin added a third finger, using her weight to push deep inside and send Sadie over the edge. Fireworks burst behind her eyes and Sadie flooded Fin with her wetness. She was still pumping inside her, oblivious to the fact Sadie had already come.

"Stop, Fin," she managed to gasp, but she could feel another orgasm beginning to pulse again already.

"You can come again. Ah fuck, Sadie, I need you to come again." Fin groaned without breaking the rhythm. Instead she ground herself even harder against Sadie, the hand that held Sadie to the table tightening almost painfully, and God help her, it was turning her on.

Sadie had never imagined this, but the rough was thrilling her in a way she hadn't experienced since they met. She loved having sex with Fin, but they hadn't fucked—properly just fucked—since the beginning. And not only that, but there was no tenderness to Fin now, no gentleness or care. There was this…animalistic fucking was the only way she could describe it, and now she was coming again and she was making noises that had never come out of her mouth before. Grunts and pants and moans as she pushed down and fucked Fin's fingers relentlessly.

She was still coming down from her second orgasm when Fin pulled out of her without warning, her other hand letting go of Sadie's. Fin gripped her hips hard, painfully, and Sadie knew it would leave bruises. She pulled Sadie against her, thrusting her hips against Sadie's backside, the slap of wet flesh and Fin's grunts the only sounds. Fin cried out once, then collapsed on Sadie's back, her weight pushing her into the table, the edge uncomfortable against her battered pussy.

Sadie's chest began to tighten as her mind rebelled at the sensation of being trapped, unable to shift Fin's weight off her.

"Fin," she said desperately, hoping her wife could hear her.

Then Fin was gone, and Sadie took in a deep breath, two deep breaths. She stood up as Fin left the room.

Sadie reached down and pulled up her knickers and jeans. She fixed her hair, which had come loose from its clip. Downstairs, in the basement, the banging started again.

CHAPTER TWENTY-FIVE

"She just came in and fucked you on the kitchen table?" Rachel pretended to fan herself, then, as if realizing, pushed back in her chair. "Yuck, this table?"

"We only have one kitchen table, Rachel. Anyway I wiped it down after." Sadie pulled on her sleeves which had started to ride up. Her hips weren't the only place she was bruised.

Rachel's eyes flicked downward to her arms. She didn't miss a trick.

"Sadie. Did…I mean was it—"

"Yes. It was completely consensual. Fin would never do anything I didn't want." And she hadn't. Sadie was a willing participant. It had been thrilling and dirty and tapped into something inside Sadie she'd never examined before. Something she definitely didn't want to examine with her best friend.

Rachel nodded, not convinced.

"Rachel." Sadie sat and took her hands. "I'm an intelligent woman. I know my own mind and what Fin did—what *we* did…" How did she explain it? "I liked it."

"What about the bruises you're trying to hide?" Rachel's voice was hard. Her lawyer voice.

Sadie sighed. "We had rough sex. I wore this so the children wouldn't ask any questions."

"Right. So can I expect to see you bruised more often?"

Rachel didn't get it. Sadie wasn't sure if she did either, completely. She knew she had wanted it, though. "Rachel. Can we talk about something else please? You're starting to annoy me with all your judgement." Sadie withdrew her hands.

"I'm not judging you. I'm concerned about you—about *both* of you. You've been through hell and now Fin is…I don't know how to describe it. Not herself. She looks like shit. Then I come back with the children, and you tell me she fucked you on the kitchen table, *bruised* you, and then disappeared without a word."

Put like that, it didn't sound too great, Sadie had to admit.

"When we were together," Rachel continued quietly, "you never wanted sex like that."

Sadie looked at her friend. They rarely talked about the time they were a couple. The relationship only lasted a few months before they decided they were better off as friends. There had never been that spark with Rachel like there was with Fin. They got on and had the same interests, but Sadie never had the urge to rip her clothes off, or to let Rachel take her as she'd let Fin earlier.

"Rachel, *I* didn't know I wanted sex like that until I was face down on the kitchen table." Something about that description struck them both as funny and they started giggling. The tension broke.

"I love you, Sadie. I just want to look out for you," Rachel said, sobering.

"I know, and I love you too."

"I mean…I *really* love you, Sadie."

"I *really* love you. You're an amazing friend to me. Believe me when I tell you nothing happened between me and Fin I didn't want. Okay?"

Rachel nodded. It seemed like she wanted to say something else, and she hesitated before raising one eyebrow. "Face down on the kitchen table, eh?"

They both started laughing again.

❖

Fin carried one of the boxes upstairs and into the kitchen. She could hear the two of them in there giggling like idiots. They were probably pissed already. Fin sighed and shook the mean thought from her head. Why was she bothered about that? Sadie and Rachel always drank too much wine when they got together, and she'd never cared before.

She never cared before they bought this place and all the work that came with it. Now Fin was doing all the work of making it nice for them, while her wife got pissed and did nothing. She hadn't even been in the basement, hadn't seen how fascinating it was.

Fin banged the box down on the kitchen table between Sadie and Rachel.

"Hey!" Rachel cried, lifting her glass of wine out of the way. "Careful, Fin."

"God forbid I spill your precious wine, eh, Rachel?" Fin wiped the sweat from her forehead. It was hot in the basement and she was soaked.

"Is everything okay, darling?" Sadie asked cautiously.

"Fine. While you two have been sitting up here, I've been down there working all day," Fin said.

"Not *all* day." Rachel winked at her, and Fin couldn't explain why, but she had a strong urge to punch that smug grin off her face.

"What the fuck does that mean?" Fin snapped.

"Fin!" Sadie stood. "Don't be so bloody rude. She was joking with you."

She saw Rachel eyeing her coolly. "Is everything okay, Fin?" she asked.

"Fine, thanks, Rachel. How are you? Still shagging your way through London?"

"Why don't you just go away if you're going to be so horrible," Sadie said, standing. "Seriously, bugger off back to the basement or something."

Fin turned without another word and left. She heard Sadie apologizing for her as she shut the door behind her.

She got to the basement door and saw Liam standing at the bottom of the stairs, worrying his bottom lip. Fin plastered a smile on her face. How much had he heard?

"What's up, mate?" She tried for a friendly tone even though she was impatient to get back in the basement.

"I had a nightmare. What's shagging?" he asked.

Fin cringed inwardly. "Something you don't need to worry about for a while yet. Come on, I'll take you back to bed." She held his hand and led him back up the stairs.

"Is it something you get when you're old? Like sore knees?"

Fin laughed. "Sort of. What was your dream about?"

"Koosh," he said quietly.

"Lucy's imaginary friend?"

"He's not imaginary," Liam said climbing back into bed. "He lives here. Floyd sees him too."

"Floyd who helps me?"

Liam nodded. "He doesn't like coming in the house because of Koosh. Koosh scares him."

Bloody Floyd, putting ideas in her son's head. She'd deal with him tomorrow—no, tomorrow was Sunday. Wasn't it? She'd deal with him on Monday.

"Don't listen to Floyd, mate."

"Koosh pushed Lucy off the playset."

Fin ground her teeth. "Who told you that? Your mother?"

Liam shook his head. "No, Lucy. She doesn't want to play with him any more."

"Come on, lie down." Fin stroked his head and tucked him in. She'd deal with fucking Sadie tomorrow as well. Using the kids like that wasn't right—she'd obviously told both of them her stupid story about Lucy being pushed. "Night, mate."

"Night," Liam replied.

Fin left his door open a crack to let in some light from the hall. She was in the basement again before she remembered she hadn't asked what happened in his dream.

CHAPTER TWENTY-SIX

Fin pushed open the door and stepped into darkness. The door clicked shut softly behind her. There was nothing to light her way along the narrow passage, but she didn't need it. She knew where she was going.

She followed the stairs down, her bare feet making no sound on the cold wooden boards. They didn't even squeak. At the bottom a faint light glowed some distance away, and she walked towards it until she was standing in a long narrow room. Shelves lined one wall and were filled with books and jars and papers. In the middle was a steel table like something you might find in a mortuary—not that she had ever been in a mortuary, but she'd watched enough television.

The table was streaked with blood and it was fresh. Fin knew it was fresh because she could still smell it in the air, that coppery scent mixed in with the damp, rotten smell of the basement. Tools were discarded on the table, and they were also covered in blood. They were wicked looking and sharp and something turned over in her stomach.

Fin turned at the sound of a *whoosh*, like a boiler kicking in. A door squealed on rusty hinges. Fin walked towards the sound, further along the basement. It was the furnace she'd uncovered earlier. Except now a fire burned brightly within, letting off waves of heat. She peered through the small window in its door but couldn't see anything except flames.

In the centre of the basement was another table. This one was much larger, though, and Fin couldn't remember seeing it down here before. On it lay two lumps covered by sheets. Fin's heart began to thump in her chest. Her legs moved of their own accord towards the table, and her shaking hand lifted itself to pull away the sheets, despite her mind issuing a command to stop.

She didn't want to know what was underneath, afraid she already did. Her hand trembled, lifted the corner of the sheet, and pulled it back. She'd never met the man who lay there, but she knew him from his photograph. Lance Sherry's waxy, still face stared up at her, his eyes wide open and milky, a scream caught on his lips. She couldn't say she was sorry for how he'd ended up, though it sickened her all the same.

Fin moved along to the next sheet, more confident now she knew it wasn't her family underneath. Her hand—still with a mind of its own—lifted the sheet, and this time she did cry out.

Rachel.

Rachel lay there, her face frozen in fear. She wore a long jagged cut as a necklace, the blood long congealed and turned the colour of rust.

Fin turned at a sound behind her. It was him. Nathaniel Cushion was standing at the foot of the basement stairs. He was smiling at her. He held open his arms as if she were a child and he expected her to run into them. And dear God, she was moving towards him on legs that didn't belong to her. Any second she would reach him. He was covered in blood. Rachel's blood. Lance Sherry's blood. And she was about to walk straight into his arms—

Fin bolted upright and swallowed the scream that threatened to break free. She reached for her phone and saw the time was three fifteen in the morning. She'd managed less than four hours sleep. It seemed to be less every night now.

Fin got up from the bed, careful not to wake Sadie who slept peacefully beside her. As was now becoming her early morning ritual, she checked on the kids to make sure they were safe and in their beds, and she went downstairs.

She padded quietly down the basement stairs and flicked on the light. Satisfied no bodies or Victorian gentlemen lurked, she turned to go back upstairs. Her foot connected with something solid and it skittered underneath the wooden stairs.

Fin walked back around and crouched down, using the torch on her phone to light the area. The object landed in the corner, caught partially under a box no doubt filled with more of other people's crap.

Fin reached out and snatched the object up. She held it up to the light, and her stomach clenched. It was a scalpel and it looked new. She turned it in her hand and flicked her finger along the edge of the blade. It was sharp. She was lucky—she must have kicked the handle, because the blade was sharp enough to open up her foot.

What was going on? Was Sadie right? Was Liam right? Maybe this place was bad. She couldn't sleep, she couldn't eat. She found herself furious with Sadie for no reason and impatient with the kids. Last night she'd been so rude to Rachel, and she had no idea why. It was these dreams, these fucking horrible dreams.

Briefly, Fin wondered if she was having a breakdown. She heard Rachel ask Sadie last night after her outburst. The acoustics in the basement were funny like that—you could hear everything if you stood in the right place. By the far wall she could even hear Lucy playing upstairs in her room.

Something was wrong with this house, wasn't there?

The bulb above her head popped and went out. Fin fumbled with her phone to switch on the torch just before something hit her from behind.

Fin opened her eyes. She tried to move her legs but couldn't, because something heavy lay across them. She could sit up, though, and was relieved to see it was boxes and old furniture that had fallen across her legs—nothing catastrophic as she'd feared. She must have destabilized a pile of it yesterday.

Fin kicked out, shoving the boxes and other detritus off her legs, then stood, brushing her hands down her shorts. Her phone lay on the ground close by, the torchlight still shining, which was handy because the door had swung closed above, sealing off any light.

Fin climbed the stairs and was nearly brained when the door swung inwards. She was blinded though by the torchlight suddenly in her eyes.

"For fuck's sake, Sadie. Point that somewhere else, would you?" Fin snapped.

"Sorry, sorry." Sadie switched it off and stepped back. "I heard a loud bang and came downstairs. None of the lights are working."

"What, anywhere?"

"I tried upstairs and nothing came on."

The basement must have tripped all the lights, which was odd because most circuits were arranged floor by floor. Still, in a house this old who knew how the electrics were organized. The previous owners had been more worried about how it looked than whether anything actually worked.

Irritated, Fin reached out her hand. "Give me the torch. I'll go and have a look."

Sadie handed it over without a word. Which was just as well, because Fin really wasn't in the mood for her shit right now.

CHAPTER TWENTY-SEVEN

Fin pulled at the collar on her new shirt. The starch rubbed at her neck, and she knew she'd have a red mark tomorrow. She'd had to buy the new shirt because her old ones were too big since she'd lost so much weight.

Sadie fussed and even Fin made an effort to eat, but the weight kept falling off her. Neither of them had said the C-word yet, but Fin knew they were both thinking it. She was waiting for Sadie to suggest a doctor's visit. It would be the perfect end to a really shitty year, she supposed.

Fin sighed and tugged at her shirt again. Rose had invited them for dinner. She and the dog walker were official. Fin hadn't wanted to go—she'd barely spoken to Rose in weeks—but Sadie insisted it would be good for them.

Lately, their relationship was creaking. Fin couldn't seem to stop being annoyed at Sadie, and she had no idea why. Even the sound of her breathing in the night pissed her off. Sadie responded by nagging her even more, so that they'd had two huge fights in the last week alone. They never fought. Not properly anyway, and Fin knew it was mostly her fault, which made her even more angry.

They'd dropped the kids off at Sadie's parents. Fin waited in the car because she couldn't face Sadie's dad. The lack of sleep was making her already short fuse even shorter, and she was sure Treven Tate might be the one to light it for good.

Rose threw open the door with a huge grin on her face, which promptly disappeared as soon as she caught sight of Fin.

"Jesus, Fin, you look like absolute shit."

Leave it to Rose to call a spade a spade. "Thanks, Rose, can we come in?" Fin thrust a bunch of flowers at her.

Rose's girlfriend Janey came out of the kitchen holding a large spoon. Fin was relieved she was the one cooking. "Hey, Sadie. We didn't need to stop at McDonald's after all." She pointed at Janey. "Rose isn't cooking."

It earned her a punch on the arm from Rose, and Sadie actually laughed. She hadn't had much reason to laugh lately. Fin felt a stab of guilt.

"Hello again. I think I'm still hung-over from last time." Janey grinned.

"I think Fin definitely still is. Fin, you've wasted away. What happened? Are you sick?"

"Rose!" Janey said. "That's so rude."

Rose shrugged. "Well, look at her."

"I'm not sick, Rose." Fin glanced at Sadie who couldn't hide her worry, and there was that guilt again, poking her in the gut. "I haven't been sleeping well and work's been hectic."

Rose nodded, seeming like she would let it drop. "Well, Janey is cooking the most amazing curry for us, and it's full of butter and cream. You'll probably put at least ten pounds on before we even get to dessert."

❖

Fin huddled with Rose under the awning in the back garden. She took a deep drag of the cigarette and handed it back to Rose. The evening had gone well. Really well. Janey was as lovely as the first time she met her, and Fin had felt more like her old self tonight. Some of the warmth she felt towards Sadie had come back, along with her appetite.

"That curry was lovely. Janey is a great cook," Fin said, taking a drink from her beer.

"She's going to give you some to take home. You look like you need it."

Fin looked at her friend, took the cigarette back. "Give it a rest, Rose."

"You're such a fucking knob sometimes."

Fin grinned. "Do you kiss Janey with that mouth?"

"Kiss more than her mouth and she loves it." Rose winked salaciously and rubbed her hands together like a dirty old man.

Fin laughed and elbowed her. "You're so disgusting. I like Janey, you know. A lot. And you look happy."

"I am," Rose agreed. "You don't look very happy, though."

"I'm all right. Me and Sadie…we're going through a rough patch is all."

Rose took back the cigarette, nearly down to the butt now. "Is that all it is? I mean, you'd tell me if it was anything else, wouldn't you? Like…I don't know, if you were sick."

Fin looked at her friend, shocked to see she was welling up. "I'm fine. Christ, Rose, don't cry." Fin pulled her into a rough hug and Rose returned it fiercely.

"It's just, we haven't spoken much recently. I miss you. Then I saw you tonight and I wondered if you were sick. If that's why you weren't returning my texts or calls—"

"I've been a shit friend lately, I know." Fin felt guilty all over again. "I'm not sick. Well, I mean, I don't think I am."

Rose raised her head, sniffling. "You don't *think* you are?"

"I don't know what's wrong with me. I can't eat, I can't sleep. I'm horrible to Sadie and short tempered with the kids. I have these dreams…" Fin trailed off. She hadn't meant to say so much. Rose had a way of getting stuff out of her without even trying.

"I did wonder about you and Sadie," Rose said quietly.

"What do you mean?"

"You always look so solid. Always looking moony at each other. Always touching. Tonight you seemed different. Like it was strained between you."

"We haven't been getting on. Just a rough patch," Fin said simply.

"I used to be jealous of her, you know."

"Of Sadie? Why?" Fin was surprised.

"The way you looked at her. You never looked at me like that." Rose smiled sadly.

"Did you want me to? I mean, I know we dated, but it wasn't serious."

"Wasn't serious for you. I was in love."

Rose's gentle admission stunned her. Fin stepped away, studied Rose to make sure she wasn't winding her up.

"You never said anything."

"Of course I didn't. You didn't feel the same. I was just a fuck to you. I saw what was going to happen, so I manoeuvred you into the friendship zone." Rose did smile then. "I wanted to keep you in my life."

Fin didn't know what to say.

"Don't shit a brick, Fin. I'm not in love with you any more. I still love you, but not like that. The reason I'm telling you now is because I know you love Sadie. I knew it back then, when you talked about her, when I saw you together. So don't be a total dick and push her away. You actually turned into a decent human being after you met her."

Fin gulped down the rest of her beer. "Cheers."

"You know what I mean. You got yourself together properly. Now you have two beautiful kids. Don't fuck it all up."

"It's what Claibornes do. For over a hundred years apparently." Should she tell Rose about Nathaniel Cushion?

"What are you talking about?"

"Never mind." She'd keep it to herself. "I just meant I haven't exactly had awesome role models. Claibornes are horrible people."

"Not all of them. You aren't. Get your head out of your arse. Go to the doctor, a therapist, whatever you need to do, but sort yourself out, Fin."

Fin nodded. Smiled. She should have come to see Rose weeks ago. If anyone could pull her out of a self-pitying funk, it was Rose.

"Come on, let's go back inside. I'm cold."

Fin stopped Rose with one hand and pulled her back into a hug. She kissed her softly on the lips.

"What was that for?" Rose blushed.

"For staying in my life. I would have been lucky to have you as my girlfriend."

"No, you belong with Sadie. I'm much too good for you."

Rose darted out of her arms but not quick enough to avoid the smack to her backside. She laughed and ran for the door.

Chapter Twenty-eight

4th December 1904

I am alone. Finally. I told the neighbours my dear wife Marnie and the children were gone to America. They seemed to believe me and will believe me again in several years when I tell them they are dead. The truth is, that as we sat in the conservatory drinking tea, my dear wife and dear, dear children are laid out beneath us on steel tables. In the basement. Most people would think me a monster for doing what I did, but the fact is, they were in my way. That is all. They were a nuisance with their constant demands and needs, and so I got rid of them much like a farmer puts down poison to rid himself of rats in the barn. They were holding me back but not any more. They barely suffered. There are no more rats in my barn.

Sadie rushed into the kitchen and pulled on her shoes. She hadn't worn heels for months, and her feet didn't appreciate being squashed into them now. She gathered her hair together and used a clip to hold it. She noticed Fin staring at her with a confused look on her face. The dark circles were still under her eyes but she'd put some weight back on.

"What?" she snapped.

Fin shrugged. "Just wondered why you're all dressed up like that."

"Are you going to a party, Mummy?" Lucy asked around a mouthful of cereal.

"No, I'm going to a job interview. You knew this, Fin."

"Nope. You didn't tell me. Who's looking after the kids?"

Sadie took a calming breath and willed herself not to start shouting. They'd both been better the last few weeks, although things were still strained. "You said you would watch them. We spoke about this."

Fin shook her head. "Next Wednesday, you told me."

"No, today. It's on the fuck—It's on the calendar." She lowered her voice when Liam looked up and frowned at her. "Wednesday the twentieth. I have an interview in Cambridge."

"No, you said next week." Fin looked at her with a smug smile. Sadie wanted to slap it off.

She strode over to where the calendar hung on the wall and picked it up. She flicked it to today's date and—

Shit. It wasn't there. She flicked again and saw it wasn't in next week either. She could have sworn she'd written it down.

Fin was still looking at her with that self-satisfied grin. Sadie hadn't seen it before, but there were a lot of expressions Fin had been throwing her way lately she hadn't seen before.

"Can you watch them for me, please?" she asked through gritted teeth.

"Nope. Have to go to London in an hour to pick up a sofa."

"Can you take them with you and drop them at my parents?" Sadie knew it would be easy enough for her to do. "Please, Fin."

Something shifted in Fin's face. The smirk was gone and Sadie glimpsed her old Fin again. "Fine. Okay. I'll drop them on my way. Write it on the calendar next time."

Sadie ignored the dig. "Thank you. I have to go." She kissed the children on the head and for the first time missed Fin out.

"Have fun today and be good for Granny and Grandad." To Fin, "I'll call them on my way to the interview."

Fin nodded but didn't speak.

"Have fun at the party, Mummy," Lucy called out after her, and Sadie smiled for the first time that morning.

Sadie hunted around the console table in the hall for her car keys. They were usually in the bowl but she couldn't find them. She checked her watch. Still time, if she left now.

She rummaged around in the drawers, even pulling them out in case the keys were caught at the back. Nothing. Shit.

She opened the coat cupboard and checked her pockets, checked her handbag. Which one did she use yesterday? Didn't matter, she checked all of them.

Sadie wanted to cry. The morning started off horribly and now it was getting worse by the second. How could she get through an interview like this?

"Fin?" she called. No answer. Sadie stomped back into the kitchen. "Fin. Have you seen my car keys?"

"Nope."

Nope. She had started saying that a lot recently as well, and it was driving Sadie up the wall. Smug little shit.

She stomped back out and checked her car to see if she'd left them in the ignition. She looked at her watch again. She was going to have to ask Fin for another favour.

Back in the kitchen. "Can you please drop me at the station? I can't find my car keys."

"What do you mean you can't find them?"

"What do you think I mean? I. Can't. Find them. Even you should be able to understand that one, Fin. No big words at all."

That was a mistake. She watched Fin's eyes narrow. Liam looked between them like he was at a tennis match. Lucy was oblivious.

"Here's one for *you*, Sadie. Go. And. Fuck yourself."

Liam gasped.

"Fine."

Sadie went out into the hall again and used her phone to call a cab. Ten minutes. She might still make it if the train was on time. She tried not to think about what Liam just heard. She and Fin needed to talk. Seriously talk. They couldn't carry on like this. Not with the kids listening to them talk to each other like shit—what kind of example was that?

She would make Fin go to therapy with her. If she refused, which was likely because Fin hadn't even been to the doctor about her weight loss yet, then she would leave. She'd take the children and stay with her parents.

Sadie heard the cab pull into the drive. She stepped outside and tried not to cry.

❖

Fin was most of the way in the kitchen before she saw Sadie at the table. It would look childish if she walked out now, even though she couldn't bear to be in the same room with her.

Sadie was still dressed in her interview outfit. Fin filled a glass with water and drank deeply. "How was the interview?"

Sadie burst into tears.

For the first time in their marriage, Fin wasn't sure what to do. Ordinarily, she would have gathered Sadie into her arms, but there was a good chance she was crying because of Fin.

Fin settled for placing one hand on her shoulder. Sadie didn't shrug her off, so it wasn't something she'd done.

Fuck it.

"What's the matter, babe?" Fin moved around and pulled her into a hug. She hated to see her cry. Sadie buried her face in Fin's stomach and laced her arms around her middle.

Fin stroked her hair and rocked her gently. "Has something happened?"

Sadie leaned away and Fin wiped at the mascara which had run down her face.

"I missed the interview."

"Oh." So it was sort of to do with her. "What happened?"

"There was a problem with the trains. They were delayed half an hour."

Fin felt that familiar old guilt settle inside her. She could have taken Sadie to her interview—she'd had time. But no, she had to be an arsehole and she wasn't even sure why.

"Can you rearrange it?"

Sadie nodded. "I'm not crying about just that."

"Oh."

"What's happening to us, Fin? You're horrible to me, I'm horrible to you. We're both so bloody horrible to each other. Why?"

Fin gulped. Sadie looked so sad and so confused. "I don't know." She sat down heavily in the chair beside her. "Maybe we need a holiday? There's still a week of half-term left."

"We don't need a holiday, Fin. We need to see a therapist. I want you to come with me."

Fin sucked in a breath. "Okay."

"Really?"

"You didn't think I would?"

"I wasn't sure. I know you hate that sort of thing."

"What sort of thing?"

"Emotions." Sadie smiled. It wasn't a dig.

Fin grinned. "It's worth a go. Rose told me I needed to get my head out of my arse. Maybe this will help."

Sadie started to laugh but stopped suddenly at the sound of a loud bang. She had just enough time to pull Fin out of the way before the light fitting crashed down, splitting the dining table almost in two.

Chapter Twenty-nine

The sound of the crash brought Liam running in from the other room where Sadie had sent him and Lucy to watch a film. Fin gathered him up in her arms, something she hadn't done for a long time. She wasn't sure if it was more for his comfort or hers.

The light fitting had landed inches from where she'd been sitting and probably would have killed her if Sadie hadn't pulled her back. Jesus.

"We're fine, we're fine." She spoke into his soft hair as she rocked him.

Liam pulled back in her arms and studied her intently. "You look scared."

Fin laughed shakily. "Yeah, I am a bit scared. And I'm lucky Mummy pulled me out of the way of the light." She put him back down on his feet. "I think I'll be having a serious word with the electrician."

"It wasn't her fault, Mum," Liam said, his big brown eyes serious. "It was the house."

Fin bit back the harsh words on her lips. "It wasn't the house, mate. It's just a house, and houses can't hurt people." She looked at Sadie, the words meant for her as well. Sadie looked away.

"Why don't you go back to your film? Lucy's waiting for you."

"Lucy went upstairs to play with Koosh. They're friends again."

"Great." Fin groaned. Neither she or Sadie had heard her, and when Lucy was quiet it usually meant trouble. "Do you want to go and see what's she's getting up to? I'll sort this mess out," Fin said to Sadie.

Sadie nodded. "Don't try to move the light on your own, though. I can help."

"I'll just turn off the power to the kitchen light. All the wires are exposed up there."

The last thing they needed was a fire, although Fin was starting to think it might be the answer to Sadie's prayers. When had everything wrong in their lives started getting blamed on the house?

More to the point, why was everything going wrong in their lives?

Fin picked up a dustpan and brush and began sweeping broken glass from the bulbs that smashed. She and Sadie had always been so solid. Even the stuff with Lance Sherry hadn't put a dent in their relationship. Sure, they argued sometimes—they weren't perfect—but they never did it in front of the kids, and Fin knew she'd never done anything like how she'd handled Sadie's job interview before. She didn't want Sadie to get a job, and she didn't even know why. It was a feeling which was almost foreign to her.

Their whole relationship, Fin was proud of Sadie's career. Of course there were times she felt resentment that the bulk of childcare or housework fell to her, but Sadie worked so hard to get where she was, and Fin loved being with such a successful woman. Until they came here.

Maybe it was having Sadie home more, taking on more of the stuff with the kids that she didn't want to lose. Perhaps somewhere inside she'd been resentful this whole time and just hadn't realized it. Fin sighed and tipped broken glass into the bin. Something inside her had changed, and she didn't understand it or know how to take it back. It wasn't the house or Sadie's job—it was Fin. That old darkness from years before was rising again, and she wasn't sure if she could turn it back. Meeting Sadie and Rose and having the kids had pushed it away, and Fin thought it was gone for good.

Maybe what she'd said to Rose at the dinner party was true. Claibornes always ended up fucking things up, and she'd been deluding herself to think otherwise.

Sadie called from upstairs and roused her from her dark introspection.

❖

Sadie met Fin at the top of the stairs. "Don't get angry," she said.

"What's happened?" Fin asked and Sadie noticed she hadn't agreed not to get angry.

"Lucy's made a mess in her bedroom." That wasn't quite the truth, but with the way Fin was behaving lately, Sadie wasn't sure about telling her the extent of it. She was shocked herself. Lucy had always been rambunctious and slightly heavy-handed, but she'd never before engaged in the kind of destruction she'd unleashed on her room. Sadie still wasn't sure how she'd managed to do it so silently.

"What sort of mess?" Fin tried to move around her, but Sadie blocked her path.

"I mean it, Fin. No angry outbursts."

"Fine, fine. It's obviously pretty bad. Where's Lucy?"

Sadie had sent her to wait in Liam's bedroom after coming upon her sitting on the floor amongst the mess, looking just as surprised as Sadie. She probably was. Lucy wasn't one for thinking things through—she was the opposite of her brother in every way.

Sadie led Fin down the hall and opened Lucy's bedroom door. She stepped back to allow Fin inside first.

"Jesus Christ." Fin sounded in awe rather than mad. "What the fuck did she do in here?"

Lucy's mattress had been pulled from the bed and slashed. The chest of drawers Fin built for her was pulled over and the contents strewn around the room. Broken toys and torn clothes littered the floor. The worst part, though, were the crayon drawings of penises all over the walls. They were hideous and graphic and Sadie had trouble believing their three-year-old child would have the knowledge—let alone the ability—to draw the detailed renderings.

Fin turned to her, wide eyed and horrified. "Is this my fault?" she asked, and for the first time in ages, Sadie wanted to hug her.

"Of course it's not your fault."

"Are you sure? I mean, I've been particularly horrible recently—"

"Neither of us has been very nice."

"Why would she do this?"

"I don't know."

Sadie hadn't asked her yet. Besides, Lucy was only three and the chances of her being able to articulate her feelings wouldn't be high.

"It's some sort of reaction to the stress, maybe? Of us fighting all the time?"

"Maybe," Sadie agreed. "But, Fin, she's three and she's got a broken arm. How did she manage to push over a chest of drawers? How would she know what a penis looks like when it's…when it's…you know?"

"You think Liam helped her?" Fin stepped further into the room and began picking up the detritus on the floor. "Look, her unicorn." Fin held out the stuffed toy Lucy had had since birth. It went everywhere with her, and now it was destroyed. The stuffing was torn out and the horn ripped off.

"I doubt he would do something like this."

"Let's go and ask her," Fin said.

In Liam's bedroom, Lucy sat on the bed, her broken arm resting in its bright purple cast across her lap. She looked scared.

"Lucy, we need to talk to you," Fin said gently and sat beside her.

"I'm sorry, Mummy," she replied quickly, looking between the two of them. "Koosh is sorry too."

"Lucy, why did you do it?" Fin asked.

"*I* didn't. Koosh did."

Sadie came to sit on the other side of her. "Lucy, you need to tell the truth."

"Koosh said, play hide-and-seek. I hid. Koosh did it when I was *hiding*."

Sadie sensed Fin struggling to hold her temper. "Koosh isn't real."

Lucy nodded her head vigorously. "He is real. He's my friend."

"Lucy." Fin's firm voice made Lucy flinch. "You're already in trouble for what you did. Lying to us is only going to make things worse. Now tell us why you did it."

Lucy hung her head and began to cry. She tried to crawl into Sadie's lap, but Sadie held her back. "No, Lucy. You've done a really naughty thing. Do you understand?"

"It's not me!" she suddenly screamed. "Koosh did it!" She jumped up from the bed and ran out of the room. Fin went to follow, but Sadie held her back. "Hang on a minute."

"What? So she can go and trash another bedroom, then blame it on her imaginary friend?"

"What if she's telling the truth?" Fin looked at her like she was an alien. Like she'd lost her mind. "I mean, what if she thinks this Koosh did do it?"

"You mean she's schizophrenic? Come on, Sadie."

"No, I don't mean that."

"What do you mean then?"

Sadie wasn't sure. There was something in this house. She'd seen it push Lucy from the playset outside. She didn't believe in ghosts or demons, but there was something here, and it was bad.

How did she tell Fin that, though? Fin, who flipped out at the slightest mention that the house wasn't anything except amazing?

"I just don't want you to fly off the handle."

"I don't think I've done anything of the sort so far. Jesus, Sadie, do you always have to make me out to be such a fucking monster?"

Fin stood and left the room too.

Sadie sighed. She felt like crying. Her family was falling apart, and there didn't seem to be any way to stop it. Maybe they all needed therapy. If the horrible drawings on Lucy's walls were anything to go by, she certainly did. All the same, Sadie wasn't sure if it had been Lucy. Maybe this Koosh was some kind of manifestation of the badness in the house. That was what she had wanted to say to Fin but was too afraid. And since when was she afraid to voice her fears to Fin? Fin, who was becoming angrier by the day and less and less like the sweet woman she'd married.

Something poking out from the side of Liam's wardrobe caught her attention. It looked like a sheet. Sadie stood and went over to the wardrobe. She pulled it out.

It was a sheet from Liam's bed. She recognized it as being from part of a set of racing car bed sheets Fin bought him for his last birthday. It was damp and crumpled. She sniffed it and found it smelled faintly of urine.

Sadie sat back on the bed with the sheet clutched in her hands and struggled not to cry. Liam was wetting the bed, and instead of telling her, he was hiding the sheets down the side of his wardrobe.

Everything was such a mess, and she had no idea how to fix it except by leaving this house. This horrible, evil, fucking house.

She started to cry.

❖

Fin stood over the mortuary table, dull and rusted in places. Lance Sherry lay with his eyes closed, and a single drop of blood hung suspended from his nostril, defying gravity.

"The first cut is the hardest. It gets easier after that." The voice came from behind her. Nathaniel Cushion. He sounded kind and encouraging, like he was teaching her to ride a bike without stabilizers for the first time. "I suppose it could be compared to that, yes," he said again.

He could read her mind. It didn't make sense, but this was a dream and she supposed anything was possible in a dream.

"I don't want to do it." She cringed at the whine in her voice.

"You must. He deserves it. Who would care?"

"Sadie would care."

Suddenly, he was behind her. His breath was hot on her neck, scalding. "She doesn't love you any more."

Fin turned with the scalpel raised. "Shut up. We're going through a bad patch, that's all."

He grinned, and he reminded her of Uncle Finlay. Of a lizard. "She doesn't think you're good enough. Her family don't think you're good enough. Her friends don't think you're good enough. Show them you are."

"No. It's only a dream. I'll wake up in a minute and you'll be gone."

"I'm always here. I'll be waiting until you change your mind. You can't fight your destiny, and that *family* is holding you back. You'll see."

Fin woke up. Her hand was clenched in a fist as though she still held the scalpel. She turned her head to see Sadie sleeping peacefully beside her. She got up quietly and went downstairs.

Fin booted up the computer and searched for genealogy websites. She found one which looked reputable and began her search.

Three hours later and she leaned back in the chair, absently reminding herself to fix the squeak. There it was on the screen in black and white—or rather in the website colours. It hadn't taken long or even much effort to show her link to Nathaniel Cushion, and part of her protested at that. Shouldn't there be some great revelation or uncovering? It appeared not. The wonders of technology, some names, and a few birthdates. He was her great-great-grandfather through her father's line. It appeared that *her* great-grandfather, Finlay Cushion, changed the family surname, which made sense considering what his father was hanged for.

Fin wasn't sure what to think or what to do. It seemed a strange coincidence she ended up in the house Cushion built, she dreamed about him, and Sadie was convinced the place was bad. Fin was lost. She didn't believe in ghosts or hauntings or any of that other nonsense. A house couldn't be bad—it was only bricks and mortar. But Sadie was so insistent. And Fin was so tired.

She scrubbed her eyes with her fists and yawned. If she could just get a good night's rest, she'd be able to think clearly. She'd be able to make sense of this and separate out the superstitious nonsense from the facts. But she was exhausted.

Fin cleared her browser history and shut the machine off. She lay down on the sofa and hoped to get a few hours' sleep before Lucy woke up.

CHAPTER THIRTY

S adie dragged one of the boxes through the hall and into the kitchen. Fin had squirreled them away in the basement and Sadie was curious to learn what was so interesting about them. She spent all her free time down there going through the contents. When Fin wasn't in the basement, she'd been busy with work, and Sadie had hardly seen her lately. In a way she was relieved and suspected Fin was staying away on purpose.

After their brief truce, things had pretty much gone back to the constant bickering and rows. Thankfully, they'd managed to keep it away from the children, but Sadie knew they weren't stupid and had both picked up on the terrible atmosphere in the house.

Fin hadn't mentioned therapy again, and every time Sadie brought it up, she fobbed her off with *later*, or it just started another argument. Sadie was beginning to think it might be best if she went to her parents for a while. Perhaps the time apart would be good for both of them. She refused to consider it might be the start of a formal separation yet.

What was in these bloody boxes? Fin told her there was tons of junk left down in the basement, and while she'd moved out most of the old and broken furniture, these remained down there, pushed into a corner. Sadie opened the flap on one and peered inside. It looked like documents and old photos.

Intrigued, Sadie sat cross-legged in the hall and pulled out a handful of the stuff. The first photo she came to sent shivers up her spine.

Sadie's first thought was: *What was Fin doing dressed up in Victorian garb?* At closer inspection she saw it wasn't Fin at all, but a man who looked remarkably like her. He sat on a chair, striking a pose common for the times. No smile, and his head angled slightly away from the camera. Sadie touched her finger to the photo and then pulled away sharply. Her finger tingled unpleasantly.

She looked at the man again and was filled with a sense of dread. This man was not a good man. She wondered at his link with Fin.

Sadie picked up a couple of the documents from the box and saw that they were from a ledger and detailed costs for building materials. A neat hand had filled up several columns for things that were familiar to her: bricks, stone, cement, and slate. Beside them were prices in a currency long since extinct.

She guessed they dated to around the Victorian period, and that would make sense with the photograph. They'd never really looked into the history of the house, but Fin told her the house was built around the late 1800s. Could this be the man who'd built it? And why did he look so much like Fin?

Now that Liam was in school full-time and Lucy half days, Sadie had a lot of time to go through all these boxes. Perhaps this would help to settle her that the house wasn't evil or haunted or whatever she was afraid of—even she wasn't quite sure.

She dragged the box back into the kitchen with the others and began sorting the contents. She pulled out another sheaf of documents which looked as though they belonged together in a ledger. These weren't for building materials though. At first, she was puzzled, not quite understanding what she was looking at. When she flicked to the next page, it became clearer and horrifying. The pages detailed the sale of cadavers to various medical facilities in London and beyond. There were hundreds listed in the handful of pages.

How did someone get hold of so many dead bodies, even back then? The answer was quite clear. Someone who'd lived in this house—perhaps the man in the photo—had been a bodysnatcher or worse.

Sadie flicked through the documents and photos, hoping to find a name. Page after page, she found nothing to indicate who had written the awful ledger. She stopped when she came across a photograph. Again, it showed the man from the previous photo, but this time he was joined by what she assumed were his family. A woman and two boys stood in front of what she recognized as her house.

Like the first photo, this one filled her with a sense of dread. She picked up another picture. This one only had the woman in it—she guessed she was the man's wife. She was posed on a chair, and on closer inspection, Sadie saw she was slumped slightly to the side, and the chair was propping her up. Her eyes were closed. With cold realization, Sadie knew the woman in the photo was dead.

❖

"It was common back then," Rachel said.

Sadie called her after finding that awful photo. "Common? Are you joking?"

"No. Lots of people had pictures taken of or with dead relatives. The Victorians were a weird bunch."

"What about selling the bodies?"

"Common, as well. Obviously, illegal to dig them up, but it was rife. Look, Sadie, what's going on?" Rachel's voice was gentle over the phone.

"It freaked me out. How would you have felt, finding that stuff?" Sadie hadn't told her about the man who looked so much like Fin.

"It's weird, but I don't understand why you're getting your knickers in such a knot."

Sadie was a bit embarrassed. She'd called Rachel in tears. What was wrong with her? "You're right—it was just a shock."

"Of course. Look, what are you doing this weekend?"

Sadie was dreading the weekend. It would mean extended time spent with Fin. She felt horrible for thinking it. "We don't have any plans." Except for more arguments, she thought bitterly.

"Why don't you come down on Friday night? A few of us are going out. There's people from your old chambers too. It'll do you good."

Perhaps it was exactly what she needed. A night out in London with her friends, like the old days. God, she missed her old life. "Sure. Why not? Fin can watch the children."

"Excellent. You can stay at mine, and we'll go shopping in the morning—if we're in a fit state."

They spoke for a little longer, and by the time she hung up, Sadie felt much better. It was this creepy old house and its weird former inhabitants. A night back in her old life was exactly what she needed.

CHAPTER THIRTY-ONE

Sadie ignored the exaggerated pleas of Kate and Jack who were trying to keep her on the dance floor and made her way over to the table Rachel had reserved them. She plonked down into a seat and drank deeply from her glass of wine. What she really needed was water, but there was none in sight, and she was already most of the way to drunk.

Rachel leaned over and spoke directly into her ear to be heard above the loud thumping bass. "Enjoying yourself?"

"God, yes!" Sadie shouted into her ear. "It's been ages since I've had fun."

Rachel leaned in again. "What did you say?"

"I said—" Sadie shook her head and gestured to the exit. You couldn't hear yourself think in this club, and Sadie pushed away the realization she was getting old.

Outside, Sadie breathed the clean cool air deeply. The weather still hadn't turned, and it was pleasantly warm with a light breeze that dried the sweat on her skin.

"You seem happy," Rachel said.

"I am. I'm so pleased I came."

Rachel nodded. "You haven't seemed very happy lately."

Sadie wondered how much to say. She hadn't told Rachel the extent of her problems with Fin, and she wasn't sure why. Maybe because part of her had always thought Rachel looked down on

Fin. Sadie also knew Rachel was quite close to her father, and any indication of trouble in paradise would get straight back to him. And wouldn't he just love that bit of news?

Tonight, though, Sadie was drunk, especially since the fresh air had hit her. "I think Fin and I are going to split up," she blurted out.

Rachel looked taken aback for a moment. Ever the lawyer, she recovered quickly. "Why?"

Sadie shrugged. She could feel a sob working its way up her throat. "We haven't been getting on."

"There must be more to it than that, Sadie. Though, I can't say I'm surprised."

"What do you mean?"

Rachel hesitated and Sadie knew she was calculating how much to say.

"Look, I'm not like your dad. I *like* Fin, but I always thought…"

"What?"

"That she was beneath you, somehow."

Sadie was annoyed. Whatever her problems with Fin, she certainly wasn't in any way above her. "That's a terrible thing to say, Rachel."

"I know, I'm sorry. It's the way I feel. You're a successful lawyer—or you were until she dragged you out into the boonies."

"She didn't drag me anywhere."

"She took advantage of the fact you weren't yourself and convinced you country life was the way to go. Now look—you have no job, you live in the middle of nowhere, and you aren't happy."

Despite the cruel things Rachel was saying, Sadie saw some truth in them. She wasn't happy. She hated the house and she missed working.

"You aren't arguing with me," Rachel said.

"You're right. I'm not happy living in the house so far from town. I do miss work. None of it's Fin's fault, though."

"Okay. Look, I probably said too much anyway. I didn't mean to bash Fin, it's just…I love you Sadie."

"I know." Sadie pulled Rachel into a hug. "I love you too."

"It's because I love you that I've tried to bite my tongue as far as Fin is concerned. But maybe I shouldn't have." Rachel slipped her arms around Sadie's waist.

Sadie broke Rachel's hold on her and stepped back. "What's that supposed to mean?"

"I don't want to upset you but, well, frankly I'm surprised this marriage lasted as long as it did. I always wondered if that was why she saddled you with two kids. She probably knew it was the only way you'd stay with her."

"How dare you." Sadie was surprised at how calm her voice sounded, while inside she boiled. "You're supposed to be my friend. You're supposed to *commiserate* with me, *support* me. How *dare* you say that about my children. Saddled? Fuck you, Rachel. Fuck. You."

❖

Fin put down the wallpaper steamer and used the scraper to peel off a strip Lucy had defaced with penises. If it wasn't so awful, it would be sort of funny. Not that Fin had much experience, but they looked pretty realistic to her.

The kids had gone to bed early, and at a loose end, Fin decided to get started on Lucy's bedroom. It would make Sadie happy—she hated coming in here lately. She hated a lot of things to do with Fin and this house at the moment.

Fin didn't know what to do about it. She knew most of it was her fault. She was bad tempered, and she'd tried to stay out of the way as much as possible. It wasn't the answer, though. Therapy would help, but she just couldn't bring herself to go. It was stupid, but she'd grown up with people who saw stuff like that as a weakness. You went to a psychiatrist if you were a loony. She knew it was bollocks, and she knew it would probably help, but it almost seemed like admitting defeat.

And that was the stupidest thing of all. Her relationship with Sadie was getting worse, and she should be doing everything to try to save it. Loads of people had psychiatrists, and it didn't make them loonies or losers—it was only the ignorant people she grew up with that thought that, and look where they were now. Not exactly shining examples of keeping a stiff upper lip and handling your own problems.

She hadn't told Sadie about Nathaniel Cushion either. The other day she came back and knew straight away Sadie had snooped in the boxes. Everything was out of order and jumbled up. Fin was filled with a peculiar kind of rage she'd never felt for Sadie before. She managed to calm herself down, but in the back of her mind was the thought that maybe she wasn't so different from her family. If she wanted to save her marriage, perhaps telling Sadie about Cushion wasn't the wisest idea. The apple didn't fall far from the tree after all.

She also wondered if she even wanted to save the relationship, and she felt ashamed for even thinking it. She loved Sadie with all her heart and she always would, but there was something so attractive about giving up. It would mean no more visits to her parents, feeling small and insignificant. No more dinner parties with her lawyer friends looking down their noses at her—okay, that wasn't fair. A lot of them were a good laugh and never made her feel shit. She could also concentrate on the house, on getting it the way she wanted without Sadie constantly badgering her about wanting to leave.

Lost in her own thoughts, Fin didn't see what she'd uncovered at first. When the scraper hit an edge and wouldn't budge, she looked up. It was a door.

❖

Sadie turned to go back inside the club. She couldn't get away fast enough.

Rachel gripped her shoulders. "Sadie, come on. You're better than her. You'll meet someone worthy of you. Someone who'll give you what you want. A life here in London. Amazing holidays, private school for the children, and you can go back to the work you're brilliant at."

"Just stop. Stop it." Rachel stepped close and Sadie shoved her away. "Fuck off."

Rachel looked hurt and Sadie felt bad. She shouldn't have pushed her.

"I'm sorry. I was out of order." Rachel held out her hands, palms up. "Let's forget I said anything. We're both pissed. Let's pretend this didn't happen and go back inside."

"Go back inside? Are you mad? After what you said to me?" Sadie shook her head in disbelief. How could this woman be so arrogant. Who was she? How had Sadie not seen this before?

"It makes me sad to see you like this. Wasting all your potential, all your hard work, on a life you don't even want. On a woman that doesn't deserve you."

Rachel turned and walked away. It was only then that Sadie realized she was standing in a dark alley by herself. She'd gotten much better recently, but even so, that familiar panic started to claw its way up and out of her chest. She hurried in after Rachel. What a fucking mess.

CHAPTER THIRTY-TWO

Fin removed the rest of the wallpaper from around the door. It was on one of those push-release catches, and it opened without even a squeak. Fin stood staring for a moment, wondering if she should go through. She gave the door a light shove and it opened further to reveal what looked like a passage.

She'd heard of things like this before. She remembered reading a book about Catholics installing secret rooms or passages so they could pray or escape Henry VIII's ban on Catholicism. This house was built hundreds of years later, so it wouldn't be one of those.

Most likely, it was used for the same purpose as the tunnel she found. What that was, she didn't know, but she guessed this passage would somehow lead down into the basement. Using the torch from her phone, she stepped inside.

Sadie didn't feel much like staying and partying. She was supposed to stay at Rachel's flat tonight, but she supposed she couldn't do that either now. It would be too weird.

Her only choice was to pay an extortionate amount of money for a cab home, or stay with her parents. Neither was particularly appealing, but her parents were the best bet. She would need to brace herself for her dad's questions. Unless…Rose was Fin's friend, but Sadie also got on with her. Could she call Rose and stay with her?

❖

Fin followed the passage which led along the side of the house. She mentally calculated she would be at her own bedroom now, but there didn't seem to be another secret door.

The passage was narrow, and she was reminded of her dream where she walked down one exactly like this. She also remembered what she found at the end of it, and her heart quickened.

She came to a set of dusty wooden stairs that led down and into the basement as she'd anticipated. Fin hesitated for a moment, unsure of what she was about to do and sensing somehow that there would be no coming back from this. Whatever she found down there she couldn't ever un-find, and the thought struck her as odd at the same time as she knew it was true.

Fin went down.

❖

Five minutes and a phone call later and Sadie was on her way to Rose's flat. Rose had barely opened the door before Sadie was sobbing in her arms.

She was aware of Rose leading her inside and onto the sofa, although she was almost hyperventilating now and conscious of the fact she would be mortified at her outburst tomorrow.

Rose hugged her and patted her back like a baby, mumbling words of comfort. After a while, she started to calm down and came back to herself. She stayed in Rose's arms because it felt better than anything else had lately. Rose seemed content to stay that way too.

Sadie sat back and Rose's arms fell away. "What happened, Sadie? I'm really worried about you."

Rose's gentle words nearly undid her again, but she managed to keep her composure. "Everything's just such a mess."

"Okay." Rose nodded. "Why don't you start from the beginning."

Before Sadie could think about it, she told Rose everything. All of it. She told her about how she was terrified her house was evil, how she saw something push Lucy off the playset and what she'd done to her room. That Liam was wetting the bed again and hiding it. She spoke about her fears her marriage was over and that Rachel had basically called her children and her marriage a mistake. The last revelation earned a *what a rotten cow!* from Rose that made Sadie smile.

"That's it. My life is a mess. My children are disturbed and my wife hates me."

"Don't forget the part about your best friend implying your kids were a bad idea," Rose said.

"She didn't imply they were a bad idea. She said I was saddled with them. I mean, on rare occasions I do wonder what the hell I was thinking." Sadie grinned.

Rose snorted. "What are you going to do?"

"I have no idea. And I'm so sorry for bringing this to your door. I know you're Fin's friend first—"

"I am, that's true. But I hope I'm also your friend. Besides, Fin's been a bit thin on the ground lately. She doesn't return any of my texts or calls."

"She's probably avoiding you because of what's going on."

"Because she knows I'd give her a good kicking for being such a dickhead."

Sadie laughed. "It's not all her fault."

"No, it never is just one person's fault. Do you really think your house is evil?"

Sadie told her about the photos she found and the ledger entries for the sale of body.

Rose gave a dramatic shudder. "Now that *is* fucked up."

"Thanks. Rachel didn't understand."

"Rachel's a twat." Rose waved her hand dismissively. "Have you shared any of this with Fin?"

"No. Any mention of the house being anything other than paradise and she gets so defensive."

"Why's she so invested in that creepy house?"

Sadie shrugged. "She fell in love with it on day one. I didn't have the heart to tell her I wasn't keen. I've never seen her so happy—except when the children were born of course." Sadie debated whether to tell Rose about the similarity between Fin and the man in the photo.

Sadie took a deep breath and her heart beat faster. She was worried about how Rose would take this next bit of information. "I found a photo. It's from the 1800s. There's a man in it. I think he owned the house."

"And?"

"He looks so much like Fin they could be related."

Rose studied her then, obviously having her own internal debate about whether she should say something. "What are you saying, Sadie?"

"I'll sound ridiculous." She took a deep breath and let the words rush out. "What if the house is haunted by this man, and he's somehow called Fin back because they're related?"

To her surprise, Rose didn't laugh. Instead, she said, "Did I ever tell you what Janey said when we came back that night?"

"No."

"She thinks the house is evil."

"Oh."

"She told Fin she would bring her group over with their equipment if you wanted."

"I can imagine how that went down. Fin won't hear a bad word against it."

"Sadie, there's something wrong with that house. Even I picked that up. Why is Fin the only one who hasn't?"

Sadie sighed. "Because she's somehow tied to it. Whatever it is that makes the place evil, it's latched on to Fin." It was ridiculous. She was a lawyer, for God's sake, and here she was talking about ghosts and evil and hauntings. But, somehow, telling Rose about it lifted the invisible weight that had been crushing her for months.

"What are you going to do?" Rose asked her.

"I don't know." Except that wasn't completely true. Sadie thought she might have an idea.

Fin reached the bottom of the stairs and shone her torch over the room in front of her. She bit back a scream.

CHAPTER THIRTY-THREE

Fin gazed around the narrow room, eerily similar to the place in her dream. A stainless steel table dominated the middle with just enough room to walk around the sides. Bookcases lined the walls and were filled to capacity.

Her hand which held her phone shook as she shone the light on the table where scalpels and tongs and other instruments she didn't recognize, but that gave her chills nonetheless, lay. Unlike her dream, these were rusty.

To the left, the wall had been bricked off, and the rest of the basement would be on the other side with the furnace most likely at the far end. You didn't need to be Brain of Britain to work out what this place was. She'd seen enough TV to recognize a makeshift mortuary when she saw one.

Fin walked to the bookcases and shone the torchlight over some of the titles: *Pullman's Amputation Cyclopedia, Carter's Anatomy, Episodes in Human Dissection.* There were bound ledgers stuffed with loose papers she didn't dare look inside, and jars. Jars filled with a murky substance and unidentifiable lumps of something floating around inside. Her stomach roiled. You didn't need to be a doctor to guess what was in those jars.

Two floors above, her kids slept on, unaware of the horror in the basement. At some point in time this basement was used to dissect bodies—the tunnel leading to the trees made sense now.

Somehow, the police who arrested Nathaniel Cushion never found this place. It must be where he brought his victims and—

Fin wretched, struggling to keep her dinner down. *Okay, get a grip, this happened years ago.*

That wouldn't matter to Sadie. It would be just the excuse she was waiting for to clear off to her mum and dad's. It would back up her nonsense about ghosts or whatever she thought pushed Lucy off the playset. Fin couldn't blame her. Living in a murderer's house was one thing, but living in a house where people had been butchered was something else. The evidence was all around her. She'd already seen it in a dream, and now here it was in real life. What the fuck was going on? Was Sadie right? Was this place haunted? Was it bad?

Christ, she was so tired. Her brain suddenly felt like mush, and her thoughts became foggy and muddled. She couldn't deal with this now. It was just a house…just an ordinary house with… with a bad history. That was all.

They couldn't leave. Fin liked it here. Lucy liked it here. Liam and Sadie would grow to like it here or they could leave. She could fix this. There was no way they could leave this house. Not with all the money they'd sunk into it. Not with the astronomical penalty fees they'd have to pay the mortgage company if they sold.

Fin would need to think of a way to get all this stuff out without Sadie noticing. There was no way she could leave it down here like this. Even she couldn't go on about her business with that stuff in those jars.

A thought occurred to her: Would this be considered a crime scene? Granted, it was probably over a hundred years old and the murderer was dead, but did that matter to the police? Probably not. And if she got rid of all this, would she be committing some kind of crime? Of course she would. It was obvious no one had ever found this room. The layers of wallpaper over the door upstairs were proof enough. Besides, maybe they would find DNA from his victims and be able to put some families at ease. Families who didn't even know the dead—these murders were at least sixty years old, *at least.*

She needed a drink and she needed to think. She could push Lucy's wardrobe over to the other side and cover the door. Drag her feet on fixing up Lucy's bedroom. Sadie would buy it for a while. She also needed to move those boxes out of the house before Sadie looked through any more of them.

She'd put them in the workshop—keep all the incriminating evidence in one place. A place Sadie never visited.

Fin turned and went back up the stairs trying not to think about how badly she was deceiving Sadie. Or about the fact she was considering covering up a crime—if that's what it was. There could be an innocent explanation. *Yeah, right.*

When she would have turned right, back into Lucy's room, Fin saw the passage carried on. She followed it all the way round, with another door into Liam's bedroom, then past the bathroom, and finishing at the spare bedroom where she saw another door cut into the wall. The passage appeared to wrap around the house but with access from only three rooms. The three rooms, coincidentally, that all had internal vents. She looked up and saw a thin metal pipe— maybe a gas pipe?—fixed along the top of the wall and running all the way around the passage. In the other direction, it went down into the basement.

A terrible sort of horror dawned on her. Secret passages, no door handles, a metal table in a hidden basement room. Her skin prickled and a cold lump settled in her stomach. *What the fuck was this place?*

She was afraid she might know. The rooms with the vents were used to kill his victims. Jesus Christ, the whole place was a murder house.

Fin hurried back down the passage and out into Lucy's room. Downstairs, she poured herself a large neat vodka.

❖

The house was quiet when Sadie let herself in the front door. It was still early, she supposed, and depending on how late Fin let the children stay up, they might still all be sleeping.

She was grateful. She'd slept badly at Rose's flat, going over everything in her head. She'd come to the conclusion she'd give Fin an ultimatum: either they went to therapy or she was leaving. That wasn't the hard part—the hard part would be telling Fin she didn't want to live in this house any more, whether they went to therapy or not. Sadie hated this house, had grown to hate it more and more each day. To a certain extent it was probably an outward manifestation of her feelings over her marriage. But it was also just *bad*. Liam hated it too—he was wetting the bed again, for God's sake.

She'd wait until after the weekend when the children were back at school because she knew it wouldn't be a pleasant discussion, and she didn't want them to witness it.

In the kitchen, Fin had removed the light fitting and repaired the dining table as best she could. They'd have to buy a new one because the split to the wood was severe, and the surface was gouged in places where the chandelier landed.

It had been Sadie's grandmother's and was brought all the way from Trinidad in the 1950s. Her grandmother's own father had made it, and several generations of Tates had sat around it. Sadie shook her head. It was now broken beyond repair thanks to this bloody house. She only hoped her marriage wasn't in the same state.

Upstairs, a door slammed shut.

That was the other thing she wouldn't miss. Bloody doors banging shut for no apparent reason. Sadie set the kettle to boil and looked out the window. It was a shame because the area was so lovely, and she had to admit she preferred looking out on this every morning as opposed to on someone else's house backing onto theirs.

"You're home."

Sadie jumped at the sound of Fin's voice. She turned and was instantly worried. Fin looked terrible. "Fin, are you sick?"

"No. Why does everyone keep asking me that." She sat at the table and closed her eyes.

The dark circles were now almost black and she appeared to have lost weight in the twenty-four hours since Sadie last saw her.

"You don't look good," Sadie said carefully.

"I didn't sleep very well." Fin waved her hand impatiently. "How was your night?"

Sadie'd never lied to Fin before. She had never felt the need to in all their time together. Rose had promised she wouldn't tell Fin about Rachel. On the condition Sadie did. She planned to, but not today with the children home. "My night was fine. How did it go with the children?" Sadie busied herself with making tea in case Fin saw through the lie.

"Good. How's Rachel? How's everyone at your old work?"

"Everyone's fine." Sadie put Fin's tea down in front of her. When had they become so stilted around one another? "You moved the boxes."

Fin looked around as if just noticing they were gone. "I threw a load of stuff out yesterday."

"Really? All those photos and documents? I would have thought you'd want to look through them."

Fin shrugged and Sadie got the sense she was lying, but she didn't push it.

Fin stood up. "I'm going to go down to the workshop. I've got a few things to do."

"Okay."

Sadie watched her go, relieved they wouldn't have to sit and make awkward conversation any more.

She closed her eyes against the tears that welled there and prayed her marriage could be saved.

CHAPTER THIRTY-FOUR

"Come on, Liam, get out of the bathroom." Sadie banged on the door while Lucy hopped from one foot to the other beside her. "What have I told you about locking doors? Liam?"

There was no answer from the other side. "Lucy, go and use our bathroom, quickly, darling."

She put her ear against the door and heard nothing from the other side. "Liam?" Sadie banged louder. She tried the handle again and it was still locked. She was losing her patience. "Liam! I'm going to count to three, and if you—"

"Mummy?" Liam called and it sounded like he was downstairs. She went to the head of the stairs, and sure enough, there he was, standing at the bottom with a puzzled expression on his face.

"I thought you were in the bathroom?" she said, confused.

"Ages ago. I'm having cereal."

So who was in the bathroom? It wasn't Fin, because she would use their bathroom. Besides, Sadie saw her head into the basement first thing, and she hadn't surfaced since.

Behind her, she heard the sound of the bolt being slid back on the bathroom door. Before she had time to turn and see who was in there, she felt a hard shove from behind. She made a grab for the handrail but fell short. She tried to push backward on her feet, but one foot caught on the edge of the carpet runner, and then she was tumbling down the stairs.

❖

Fin looked up from her coffee, and her first thought was someone had dropped something. The sound continued, and when she heard Liam scream, she ran out of the kitchen.

Sadie was lying halfway down the stairs, her hand gripping a broken banister which had obviously prevented her falling all the way to the ground.

Fin felt sick. She could have broken her neck. Ignoring Liam who was bordering on hysterical, she went to Sadie.

"Sadie, babe, can you hear me?" Fin touched her cheek.

"I'm okay," she said, sitting up.

"Hang on." Fin scooted behind her to support her back. "Maybe you shouldn't sit up. Let me call an ambulance."

"No, I'm fine. Bruised, but fine."

Fin wasn't sure she agreed. Sadie was pale and her cheek was starting to swell. "At least let's go to the hospital."

"I said I'm fine. Just a bit bruised." Sadie stood and Fin helped to support her.

"What happened?" Fin asked.

Sadie turned to look at her then, and Fin was surprised by the anger in her face, as if Fin pushed her down the stairs.

"What happened? The same thing that always happens in this bloody horrible house!"

Fin stepped back in the face of Sadie's sudden anger.

"Something pushed me. Oh, I know you think I'm mad, but this house is fucking evil and I've had enough!"

Fin turned to look at their son who was still standing at the bottom of the stairs. "Liam, go in the kitchen."

"No." He shook his head. "I hate this house too."

Like a guttering flame, Fin's patience finally died. She turned back to Sadie. "Go, then, you ungrateful bitch. Go on, get the fuck out of here."

"Don't worry, I am. I can't stand you and I can't stand this house either."

Now they were getting to it, Fin thought. The real reason Sadie didn't want to live here. She'd poisoned their kids' minds with crap about the house being evil, but in reality Sadie just wanted out of the marriage. "The feeling is mutual. I hate you and I really hate your fucking father. So get out of my house, you conniving, vicious bitch."

Fin didn't realize she was screaming until she was standing with her face in Sadie's, gripping her arms and shaking her. *What am I doing?* She let go and stepped back. At the same time, Liam rushed past them, sobbing, and Fin felt her world crashing down. Lucy stood at the top of the stairs staring down at them, the same fear in her face as Sadie's.

"I'm sorry," she whispered. Her legs gave out and she sat heavily on the stairs. "You should go. Take the kids."

"I'm sorry, Fin. I can't stay here any more."

Fin nodded. It was all she could manage because if she spoke now, her voice would fail and she would start to sob.

"I'll pack a few things. We can speak in a few days."

Fin nodded again but didn't look around at Sadie. She couldn't. It would hurt.

She heard Sadie start to walk up the rest of the stairs. Fin put her head in her hands. She was so tired.

The stairs creaked as Lucy came down and sat beside her. She put one tiny hand on Fin's shoulder and said solemnly, "Mama's sad. S'okay. You want a biscuit?"

Fin looked at her daughter and smiled. "Yeah, let's both have a biscuit, shall we?"

Fin picked her up and carried her into the kitchen, but her steps faltered when she saw what was on the kitchen table. It was a photograph of the Victorian gentleman. She hadn't put it there. Lucy pointed to it and said, "Koosh."

"What?" Her own voice seemed to come from far away. "That's Koosh. My friend."

Fin gently lowered her to the ground. Her heart was beating and she felt sick. "What do you mean, Lucy?"

Lucy walked over to the photo and picked it up. Fin quashed the urge to knock it out of her hand. "It's Koosh. See?" She held it up for Fin's inspection.

"That's your friend who made you mess up your room? The one you play monster with?"

"I don't play monster with Koosh no more." She shook her head vigorously. "Too scary."

Fin sat down and tried to process this information. Nathaniel Cushion was appearing to her daughter? Could it be possible? It was all too much. She felt her poor tired brain feebly grasp at more excuses and more denials about this place. The truth was plain, wasn't it? Everyone but her thought this place was bad. She had the fucking evidence in the basement, in the walls, and running through the blood in her veins. What was she going to do?

Her phone rang and she fumbled around in her pocket for it. "Hello?"

"Fin?" It was DC Helen Lyle and Fin's heart sank even further.

"Yeah. What's happened?"

"I've been trying to get hold of Sadie, but her phone is going to voicemail."

"She's upstairs. What's wrong?"

There was a beat of silence, then, "Lance Sherry escaped police custody."

Fin was numb. All she wanted to do was lay her head down on the kitchen table and go to sleep. Possibly forever. Instead she asked, "When?"

"About an hour ago. He was complaining of chest pains. We transported him to hospital and he got out his bathroom window."

"Shit."

"I know. We're sending a car over to your place now. It'll stay with you until he's rearrested."

"There's no point. You should send it to Sadie's parents' house. That's where she'll be staying."

"Oh. I'm sorry to hear that."

Yeah, so was she. Really sorry. "I'll tell Sadie. Please find him."

"We will."

Fin hung up. She couldn't believe it. Things were going from bad to worse. A month ago she would have been shouting down the phone at Helen Lyle, but it seemed all the fight had just gone out of her. She couldn't sleep or eat, her wife was leaving her, and she couldn't summon the energy to do anything about it.

Sadie screamed her name from upstairs. Once. Twice. All the energy came rushing back suddenly. Fin looked at Lucy. "Stay here."

Lucy nodded.

Lance Sherry wasn't taking any chances this time, and he wasn't hanging around. After giving the police the slip, he'd headed straight to his mum's house. She was at work but kept a spare key under a fake rock in the front garden. It was amazing how stupid people were.

He let himself in and changed clothes. He took his stepdad's car keys because he wouldn't be home until late. Lance was leaving for good. Back to Spain and then maybe Portugal, depending on what he fancied. Just one loose end to sort out first.

One particular lawyer bitch who was the source of all his problems.

He found a suitable knife for the job in his mum's kitchen. He took a couple of practice jabs imagining the bitch's soft flesh yielding when he stuck it in. Again. And again. And again.

By the time he'd finished with her, they wouldn't recognize her. He'd make sure he cut that beautiful face to ribbons. That smirking superior fucking face.

Lance let himself out of the house and got in the car. At this time of day, it shouldn't take more than an hour to get there.

❖

Upstairs, Sadie was hammering on Liam's bedroom door. Fin saw her pull back and kick it hard but it wouldn't budge.

"What's going on?" She held Sadie's shoulders and turned her to face her. Sadie's eyes were wild.

"He's in there and I can't open the door."

Fin turned to the door. "Liam! Liam, open the door."

"No, Fin, it's not Liam. It's *him*."

Fin knew who she meant, and instead of disagreeing she ran into Lucy's room. Fin hefted the wardrobe aside, unmindful of the way it teetered then crashed to the floor. She opened the hidden door and turned right towards Liam's room. The hidden door to Liam's room was wallpapered on the other side but it tore away easily enough.

Fin pushed through and saw Liam lying unconscious on the floor. She gathered him up into her arms and went back the way she'd come.

As she carried him back into the hall, she shouted at Sadie to call an ambulance and threw her phone to her. She put him on the floor and felt for a pulse. He was so pale.

She was relieved to see he was breathing. "He's alive. He's okay."

Liam's eyelids fluttered and he sighed deeply, almost as if he were asleep. "You're okay, mate," she whispered, stroking his face.

Sadie knelt beside her. "The ambulance is on the way."

"Okay. Good."

They both knelt there, watching their child.

"Once he's okay, I want to know how you got in his room."

"I—"

"Not now, Fin. Later." Sadie didn't look up. "You can tell me what you know about this house and haven't told me."

"Yes, I will. I'll tell you everything."

CHAPTER THIRTY-FIVE

Sadie stood outside the entrance to the hospital and checked her phone. There were three missed calls from Rachel. She'd left one message, which Sadie only partially listened to. At the moment, Rachel was low on her list of priorities.

Liam still hadn't woken up. All his tests came back normal, and the doctors thought he must have had a fit of some sort. They said he was sleeping, and all they could do was wait for him to wake up.

So they waited. Her parents came for a while and took Lucy with them when they left. Fin refused to leave Liam's room. Sadie knew she felt responsible for what happened and part of Sadie couldn't help but blame her either.

They hadn't yet talked about how Fin knew a way into his room—though she was grateful she did. Fin told her about Sherry escaping police custody, but she couldn't think about that right now. All she could see was her little boy lying in a hospital bed in a sleep no one could wake him up from.

She looked up as a woman came to stand beside her. The woman smiled kindly and offered her a packet of cigarettes.

Sadie shook her head. "Thanks, but I don't smoke any more. Although you have no idea how much I wish I did right now."

The woman grinned. "It's a horrible habit. And actually doesn't calm me down all that much anyway."

"The first time I met my wife, we stood on the balcony smoking cigarettes and drinking cheap vodka all night."

Sadie felt the tears come and was horrified. She hated crying in front of strangers, but she couldn't seem to stop herself.

To her surprise, the woman dropped her cigarette and pulled Sadie into a hug. Sadie held on and started crying harder, great hiccuping sobs that shook her body.

The woman rubbed her back and rocked her from side to side. "I'm so sorry," Sadie managed to say when she could catch her breath.

"Don't be silly. Sometimes it gets to be too much."

Sadie laughed but it came out more as a sob, and just like that she was off again, crying into a stranger's shoulder.

Lance Sherry parked the car in a lay-by near the bitch's house. He walked from the opposite side of the property, coming at it from the field behind, where he had less chance of being seen. He didn't have the luxury of observing their schedule as he usually did when he was planning on breaking into a house. He hoped the small group of trees would be enough to hide him while he watched their place for a while.

By his reckoning, he had about four hours until his stepdad got home. The chances were he wouldn't notice the car missing straight away because he really only used it at weekends. Lance had to allow for the possibility he would, though, so he'd have to be quick about this.

From where he hid, there didn't seem to be much going on at the house. Two cars were parked out front, so he assumed the bitch and her girlfriend were inside. He knew she had kids, and he hoped they would be at school. He didn't fancy the idea of killing kids. He wasn't a monster.

From what he knew about the bitch, the kids were small, so he could probably lock them in a cupboard or something, fuck what the Man wanted him to do. He wasn't in charge any more.

Lance was getting sick of him anyway. He'd keep to his promise of leaving the other woman alone. Something told him crossing the Man would be a mistake.

He was about to step out from the trees when a car pulled into the drive. A woman got out and went to the front door. She was all dressed up in a business suit, and Lance guessed she was one of the bitch's friends.

She knocked on the door and waited. She knocked again, then pulled her phone out and glanced at that. Was the bitch expecting visitors? It would put a crimp in his plans if she was.

He backed himself to take on two of them, but three against one? Probably not.

He waited for a bit longer, and then something interesting happened. The woman knocked on the door again, then pushed it. It opened. The bitch had left it unlocked.

Lance smiled as the woman went inside.

Fin held Liam's hand and willed him to wake up. He really did look like he was just sleeping. His eyes moved behind their lids and Fin guessed he was dreaming. "I hope they're good ones, mate," she whispered.

"I think they are. He looks peaceful."

Fin started at Sadie's voice behind her.

"Sorry. I didn't mean to startle you." She took the chair on the opposite side of Liam's bed. "Has there been any change?"

Fin shook her head. "No. He's the same." Fin looked at Sadie and saw her eyes were red rimmed and puffy. "He'll be okay. All his tests were normal."

"I know. I wasn't crying about just that."

"Oh." Fin wasn't sure what to say. She didn't want to think about the fact Sadie was leaving her.

"I was going to talk to you today. I thought I'd wait until the children were at school."

"Can we not talk about it now? I know he's asleep but he might be able to hear. I don't want him to know we're splitting up."

Sadie sighed. "Is that what we're doing, then?"

"You were packing your stuff earlier."

"I don't want to split up, Fin. I won't live in that house any more and I think we need therapy, but I'm not planning on leaving you."

Tears prickled Fin's eyes. She felt huge relief. She hadn't completely fucked things up then.

"You're right, though. Here isn't the place to talk about it all. I'm going to stay at my parents' with the children. When Liam wakes up, I'll finish getting our stuff from the house. I'm not living there again, though, so you need to decide which you want more—us or that bloody house."

As if it was even a question. "You, of course. We'll lose money on it, though."

"I don't care. It's not right. Everything that's gone on there… it's got a bad energy."

Fin smiled for the first time in ages. "You sound like Rose's girlfriend."

"Janey had a point."

"She does. I need to talk to you about the house—but not now. He might be able to hear." Fin angled her head at Liam. "Please don't leave me," she blurted out.

Sadie stood up and walked around the bed. Fin stood as well, and for the first time in ages, they hugged.

"I love you, Sadie."

"I know. I love you. You're nicer away from that house too."

Fin stayed quiet because she had a feeling it might be true. She didn't feel as tired as she had for ages. Her head was clearer and the resentment she seemed to hold against Sadie also went away. The house was wrong—she knew that now. They needed to get away.

CHAPTER THIRTY-SIX

L ance Sherry waited. The woman had been in there for about five minutes, and there was no sign of her coming back out yet. It was possible the bitch was in there and they were having a good old natter. He was starting to worry. He couldn't hang around forever. There was a ferry out of England tonight, and he needed to be on it.

Lance was on the verge of giving up when he saw something move in one of the top floor windows. It was the Man. It was *him*. Dressed in his weird Victorian clothes. He looked down and waved at Lance, and that was strange because with the distance and the angle of the sun the Man shouldn't be able to see him so clearly—if at all.

Lance grinned and waved back. The Man beckoned him as if he was saying *Come on inside*. That was when Lance knew he would be able to get the bitch after all. The Man in the window was a sign. He'd come through for Lance. As a thank you, Lance decided he would kill the kids, like the Man wanted. It was the least he could do.

Lance stood and brushed the grass off his trousers. He walked confidently towards the house.

❖

When Liam opened his eyes, the first thing he said was that he didn't want to go back to the house. Sadie told him he wouldn't have to.

The doctors ran more tests and scans and declared him fine and healthy. When Sadie told Fin she wanted to drop him at her parents', then go back for her things and car, Fin didn't object. She was almost back to her old self, and Sadie realized just how different she was at the house. It was like every one of Fin's bad qualities was magnified tenfold. Sadie hadn't escaped the house's touch either. She thought about the way she spoke to Fin there and the language she used in front of the children and felt ashamed of herself.

She hoped Fin would come back to her parents' with her. She didn't know how she would manage alone in that house. It worried Sadie. Still, this would be the last time she stepped foot in the place. And the children were never going back in there.

❖

Lance Sherry crept into the house. He waited just inside the door, listening. He moved forward carefully and glanced into the kitchen. Empty. Although it looked like the table had taken a battering.

Back in the hall, he crossed over to the living room and saw no one was in there either.

The woman must have gone upstairs. Who wandered around someone's house uninvited? Lance almost laughed.

He ascended the stairs as quietly as possible, and at the top, he heard a thump. It was coming from down the hall. Someone was banging on a door.

He moved in the direction of the noise and could hear someone's muffled pleas. That nosy woman must have gotten herself locked in one of the rooms.

Lance thought about his options. He could let her out and kill her, but that might give the game away if someone was home—although he doubted it. Or he could leave her in there. Maybe drag something against the door just to make sure she couldn't get out. If the bitch came home and heard her banging, it would draw her upstairs where Lance would be waiting.

He made a choice. Lance walked quietly to the room the woman was trapped in. The sounds were still so muffled that he thought there must be some kind of soundproofing in there. He turned the door handle.

❖

When they pulled up in the drive, Sadie groaned inwardly. "Why's Rachel here?" Fin gave voice to Sadie's thoughts. "I'm not sure."

They got out and walked to the front door. Dread settled in Sadie's stomach, and not just because of Rachel. The house seemed to loom large over her, casting its heavy shadow over them and their lives. Fin was speaking and Sadie wasn't listening. "Sorry, what did you say?"

"I said, the door's unlocked." Fin looked at her accusingly. "Honestly, Sadie. We aren't insured if someone's broken in."

"I was in a bit of a rush, Fin," she snapped back.

Inside, she called out for Rachel but there was no response.

"Where is she?" Fin asked, sounding irritated. "It's not really on to just wander around someone's house when they aren't in."

This didn't feel right. Sadie knew Rachel, and she wouldn't stay in their house when she realized they weren't home.

It was the house. It was this bloody house. Her phone rang.

She looked at the caller display and saw it was DC Helen Lyle. "Hello?"

"Sadie. Where are you?" She sounded concerned.

"At the house. I'm collecting a few things—"

"Okay. You need to get out now."

Sadie's blood ran cold. It was funny—she'd always thought that was a stupid phrase. Now she understood what it meant. She trembled. "My friend Rachel is here."

"Lance Sherry's stepfather called us. His car is missing. We put out an ANPR and the vehicle was spotted heading along the M11 about an hour ago. It took the turn-off for your place."

"Okay. But my friend—"

"We're sending a car. You need to leave *now*."

Sadie hung up and turned to face Fin. "It was Helen Lyle. Lance Sherry might be here. We need to leave."

Fin nodded. "Okay, let's go."

Upstairs a door slammed. Someone screamed.

"That was Rachel." Sadie took off towards the stairs. She could hear Fin shouting after her but she didn't stop. She took them two at a time and didn't pause at the top but continued towards Liam's bedroom. The door was shut, and just like earlier, it wouldn't open.

"Sadie! What are you doing?"

Sadie kicked at the door. "Rachel's in there."

"Are you sure?"

"Didn't you hear her scream?"

Fin drew back her leg and kicked at the door. It still wouldn't budge.

"I think he's in there with her. Please, Fin, we can't just leave her."

Fin put her ear against the door. "I can't hear anything. Are you sure you heard Rachel?"

"Yes."

"It might be him. Fucking around and trying to get us to go in there."

Sadie shook her head. "It's Rachel. We have to help her."

Fin nodded. "I'll go the same way as before."

Sadie watched as she disappeared into Lucy's room.

Behind her, she heard a click as the door to the spare bedroom opened.

CHAPTER THIRTY-SEVEN

Fin approached the secret door cautiously. She took a step and almost slipped on the wet floor.

This was a bad idea. But if Sadie was right and Rachel was trapped in Liam's room with that madman Lance Sherry, they couldn't just leave her.

Fin got to the door and put her ear against it. It was quiet on the other side. They could be in there. Maybe Sherry was threatening her to be quiet—or maybe he'd already killed her. And what could Fin do anyway against him?

She counted to three, then pushed open the door.

It was empty. She stepped inside and looked around. It looked the same as this morning, completely undisturbed.

Fin walked across the carpet and turned the door handle. The door opened easily. Sadie wasn't waiting on the other side.

Fin felt sick. Was this all a ruse just to get her up here? Did Lance Sherry have Sadie now?

Fin hurried down the hall to the spare room and tried the door. Locked. Distantly, she heard sirens, but they would be too late.

Fin hurried back down the hall and into Liam's room again, intending to go back through the passage to the spare room. If Sadie was in there, and she wasn't too late. She prayed she wasn't too late.

As soon as she stepped inside she realized her mistake. It wasn't water she'd stepped in in the passage. It was blood. Perfect red footprints marked her progress through the room.

Fin ran back through the door and along the passage. She turned the corner and hit her shoulder against one wall, making a thump, but she didn't care. She needed to get to the spare room.

This one was also wallpapered up, but it didn't slow her down as she burst through. The smell of gas hit her immediately.

She gagged and felt dizzy. Lying in the middle of the room was Sadie. Fin pulled her shirt up over her face—not that it would help—and hurried to where she lay. Still breathing. Just.

She tried the door, but this one wouldn't open. The steady hiss of gas came through the vent and continued to fill the room.

Fin took Sadie's arms and began to drag her backward into the passage. She was feeling sick now and dark spots were beginning to dance in front of her eyes.

Back in the passage, Fin dragged her all the way to the stairs. She hefted her in a fireman's carry and went carefully downward.

At the bottom, she put her down gently and looked around. The basement was the same as the last time she'd seen it, except for one thing. The door which she'd previously left unopened was now ajar.

She approached quietly and peeked her head around. Where the basement had been empty before, now the kitchen table sat in the centre. Two lumps lay on top covered by sheets. The furnace in the corner was burning brightly, obviously busy poisoning the rooms upstairs with gas. She didn't have time to think about how the system was working when it really shouldn't be.

Fin didn't want to look under the sheets, but she needed to. She had to know.

Her hand shook as she lifted the first sheet, spotted in some places and saturated in others with blood. Underneath lay Rachel. Fin choked off a sob. She was dead.

Fin moved across to the other sheet and lifted it.

Beneath it were old sheets and several stained pillows where she was expecting to find Lance Sherry.

Behind her, someone laughed. Fin looked up to see him standing there.

She'd seen a photograph of him before and was once again struck by how handsome he was. Tall with light brown hair and a baby face. He looked harmless. The knife in his hand said differently.

"He kept his word," Lance Sherry said, shaking his head with amused disbelief. "I honestly thought I was going mad, but it's real and he kept his word."

"You killed Rachel," Fin said stupidly.

Lance Sherry rolled his eyes as if she was simple. "No shit. Where's the bitch?"

"The what?"

"Sadie. Where's Sadie?"

So he hadn't seen her bring Sadie downstairs. Fin prayed she would wake up and creep back up the stairs.

"None of your business, you prick. Come on, you've got your knife, why don't you come and kill me?"

He shook his head. "No, not the deal. He's got other plans for you. I get the bitch and he gets you."

"Who gets me?"

Lance grinned and shook his head. "You wouldn't believe me if I told you."

Fin had an idea she already knew who he meant. It shouldn't be possible, and she had no idea how it was. She couldn't worry about that now. All she knew was she had to disable him if she could. He couldn't get Sadie.

She began to move around the table, hoping to get closer to the basement door where she'd left her ball-peen hammer when she'd knocked down the furnace wall.

"Why don't you just get out of here? It's not you I'm interested in," Sherry said, moving towards her.

"You must be fucking joking," she said, then launched herself at him.

True to his word, he didn't try to hurt her. He attempted to move out of the way, but she was quick and he wasn't quick enough.

Fin hit him hard and they both went down. He was bigger and stronger and managed to manoeuvre himself on top of her, pinning her down with his body weight.

"What the fuck is your problem?" He wheezed. "I'm giving you a pass, you stupid bitch."

Rather than answer, Fin spat in his face, hoping to goad him into doing something.

His face darkened, and he wiped the spit away with the heel of his hand. The hand which held the knife.

"What he wants with you, I'll never know."

Sherry drew back the hand not holding the knife and made a fist. Fin tried to prepare her body in anticipation of the blow.

It never came. Instead, Sadie appeared behind him, and Fin had just a second to register the hammer she held before it smashed down onto his head.

Sherry cried out, and Fin kicked him hard and he toppled sideways.

Fin jumped up and they ran for the stairs. Sadie pushed against the door at the top.

"It's locked."

The smell of gas was getting stronger, and Fin was worried it would reach the furnace and blow the whole place up.

Sherry groaned from where he lay on the floor, and Fin made a decision.

"Come on," she said to Sadie.

Fin led her back down the stairs and carefully around Sherry, who didn't seem to be going anywhere.

Sadie went to where Rachel lay under the sheet.

"Don't," Fin said. "It's Rachel."

Sadie seemed to sway on her feet, then got herself together. She nodded. "How are we going to get out?"

"This way," Fin said and began pulling boxes and bits of furniture away from the tunnel she'd found weeks before.

"When we get out of here," Sadie said, "I'm going to want to know how you knew all about these tunnels and passages and didn't tell me."

Fin didn't answer but she did smile.

Once she'd cleared the way, she turned to Sadie. "Go in. Just follow it all the way along."

"What are you going to be doing?"

"Dragging the ladder. Sadie, go! I'll be right behind you."

Fin got the ladder from against the wall and crawled into the tunnel. She followed Sadie through.

At the other end, Sadie looked up and saw a trapdoor. She almost sobbed in relief. Her head was pounding and she could still feel the impact of the hammer to Sherry's head. She shivered.

Fin came up alongside her, leaned the ladder against the edge of the dirt wall, and began to climb. She waited as Fin pushed up the door and daylight flooded in. She squinted against it.

Fin climbed up and over the side.

"Come on, Sadie," she said.

Sadie began to climb. As she neared the top something grabbed her ankle. She screamed. She held on with her arms and tried to use the other leg to kick, but it was no good. Whoever had her leg was strong.

Fin saw what was happening and reached down towards her.

Sadie was being dragged down. One hand lost its grip on the ladder. "Fin!" she cried.

Fin grabbed her other arm and began to pull. It felt like she was being torn apart. She would have to let go of Fin in a second.

Her hand, greasy with sweat, slipped out of Fin's, and she was dragged down and back into the tunnel. She heard Fin scream as she was pulled back at a frightening speed.

❖

Fin froze for a second. She couldn't believe what just happened. Sadie was dragged down like she weighed nothing. What the fuck got hold of her? Not Sherry, that was for sure.

Fin quickly descended the ladder and began to crawl forward. Unmindful of her hands, she practically tore at the earth, trying to move as fast as she could.

She could hear Sadie screaming and panic clenched her chest. No, no, no. This couldn't be happening.

As she turned a corner, she saw Sadie had managed to grab on to a tree root and was clinging to it for dear life.

Behind her was Nathaniel Cushion. Fin's mind rebelled. *This was not possible.* He had hold of her legs and was pulling.

Fin shuffled forward. "Let her go."

The man looked up and smiled grimly. "She's mine."

Fin grasped Sadie's arm. "Let her go."

"She holds you back. You're better off without her."

"Let her go." Except…except he was sort of right, wasn't he?

He nodded as if he'd heard her thoughts. "Yes, she holds you back."

Sadie wasn't happy here, so they were having to move. The kids hated it here because she'd poisoned their minds against it. The whole Lance Sherry fiasco was a result of Sadie's all-important career. Fin felt the tiredness seep in again, right to her bones.

He nodded again. "Yes, yes, yes. See? She holds you back. Let me have her, and you can stay here."

"Fin." Sadie's voice was quiet. "Fin, don't listen to him."

Fin glanced down at Sadie. Should she just let him have her? It would be easier. Fin could stay in the house then. Be happy.

Be free to do what she wanted to do. Her grip on Sadie's arm weakened.

Then an imagine of Liam came into her mind.

❖

Sadie looked up into Fin's eyes. In this darkness, it was hard to tell what she was thinking, but Sadie could feel it. "Please, don't let him do it, Fin. *Fin.*"

"She's a thorn in your side. She'll never be happy. Nothing you do will ever be good enough," came the voice behind her. It was a cruel voice.

"Fin." Sadie felt hopelessness setting in.

Fin raised her head as if waking from a dream.

"I said, let her go, you evil piece of fucking shit!" she screamed, and the man—the thing—recoiled as if he'd been slapped. "You can't have her. And you can't have me."

Fin's arms came towards her, and Sadie felt his grip loosen on her legs. She kicked out and connected with...nothing. Sadie turned around and he was gone.

"Come on, quick. The smell of gas is getting stronger."

Sadie began to crawl forward while Fin scuttled backward and turned.

Before too long they came to the end of the tunnel and within minutes were up and over the top.

Sadie took Fin's hand, and they ran towards the front of the house.

Fin started shouting as soon as she saw the police officers about to break into the house. Sadie realized fleetingly that he must have locked all the doors once they were inside.

"No, no! Run!" She joined Fin in shouting at them.

They paused from what they were doing and looked at her and Fin like they were mad.

"Gas, there's a gas leak." Sadie panted. "We have to go."

Fin pulled her away and they started running down the lane. She didn't look back to see if the police officers were following them.

Suddenly, it seemed as though all the air had been sucked out in a vacuum. Then Sadie was lifted off her feet and thrown forward from the force of the explosion.

It seemed like everything happened in slow motion. She hurtled through the air like a rag doll Lucy might throw. She didn't feel the impact when she hit the ground.

EPILOGUE

Fin sat in the garden chair and squinted into the sun. This summer was a heatwave, and the kids were splashing about in the paddling pool she'd gotten for them. It was much safer than a playset.

For a while afterwards, they both had nightmares. Terrible ones where they would wake up screaming and crying. Liam still got them now and again, but things were better. Things were getting better every day.

When the house exploded, Treven told her later, Liam had begun to scream and wouldn't stop. They'd called an ambulance and he'd had to be sedated. Treven said he kept saying *My Mummy is dead* over and over.

Fin closed her eyes and leaned back in the chair. She still remembered how his face came into her mind back in the tunnel. Had he managed to reach her somehow and stop her giving in to Nathaniel Cushion?

The insurance covered the loss of the house, but it couldn't bring back what mattered most. Photos, Sadie's grandmother's jewellery, Liam's first pair of shoes. All the little things you collected and put away and hoped to hand down one day.

They were making a new start, and day by day things were getting better. Her relationship with Treven had even improved to the point where they could go for a few hours without being rude to one another.

The police identified Lance Sherry by the bottom half of his face which had been found, conveniently, complete with teeth.

They'd found enough of Rachel to identify her too. Fin didn't know why she'd come to the house that day. She knew Sadie and Rachel had fought, but Rose refused to give her the details even though she was supposed to be Fin's best friend. Maybe Rachel came to apologize. Still didn't explain how she got in. Though Fin knew the house was capable of a lot of things and letting Rachel in—inviting her inside—wouldn't be beyond its ability. Or *his*.

Fin still wasn't sure she believed everything that happened. Sometimes she'd catch herself and wonder if it had been some awful dream. None of it seemed real. She sighed. She needed to stop rehashing it all the time.

She felt a cool kiss on her hot temple and smiled.

"You're going to burn." Sadie sat down beside her.

"I'm all right for a minute longer." She reached out and took her hand. She'd been doing that a lot since the explosion. It was like she needed to keep touching Sadie to make sure she was real.

The explosion had fired her into a tree, and she'd sustained serious fractures to her head. An angry red scar on her temple marked the place. She'd died in the ambulance before they managed to restart her heart. The doctors said it was a miracle she'd survived at all.

Fin lifted Sadie's hand and placed a kiss to the palm. "I love you." She'd been saying that a lot as well, but Sadie didn't seem to mind.

"And I love you. But if you don't get out of this sun, you're going to fry."

"Okay, okay. I was going to start dinner anyway."

Fin stood.

Liam screamed from the end of the garden.

Both she and Sadie were running towards him before they realized it was just Lucy taunting him with a big fat slug.

"Lucy, put it down. Seriously, that's gross." Fin shivered and Sadie laughed.

"You two are such babies," Sadie mocked them.

Lucy jabbed it at Fin, who yelped. "Lucy, I mean it." Lucy laughed and started to advance on her with the slug held out. "Lucy. *Lucy!* Sadie, tell her."

But Sadie just laughed. And now Liam was laughing too, and Fin thought that anything that made him laugh was a good thing. She took off running towards the house as Lucy chased her with the slug.

About the Author

Eden Darry lives in London with her rescue cat. When she's not working or writing, she can be found among the weeds in her allotment, trying to make vegetables grow. *The House* is her debut novel.

Books Available from Bold Strokes Books

Dangerous Curves by Larkin Rose. When love waits at the finish line, dangerous curves are a risk worth taking. (978-1-63555-353-6)

Love to the Rescue by Radclyffe. Can two people who share a past really be strangers? (978-1-62639-973-0)

Love's Portrait by Anna Larner. When museum curator Molly Goode and benefactor Georgina Wright uncover a portrait's secret, public and private truths are exposed, and their deepening love hangs in the balance. (978-1-63555-057-3)

Model Behavior by MJ Williamz. Can one woman's instability shatter a new couple's dreams of happiness? (978-1-63555-379-6)

Pretending in Paradise by M. Ullrich. When travelwisdom.com assigns PR specialist Caroline Beckett and travel blogger Emma Morgan to cover a hot new couples retreat, they're forced to fake a relationship to secure a reservation. (978-1-63555-399-4)

Recipe for Love by Aurora Rey. Hannah Little doesn't have much use for fancy chefs or fancy restaurants, but when New York City chef Drew Davis comes to town, their attraction just might be a recipe for love. (978-1-63555-367-3)

Survivor's Guilt and Other Stories by Greg Herren. Award-winning author Greg Herren's short stories are finally pulled together into a single collection, including the Macavity Award nominated title story and the first-ever Chanse MacLeod short story. (978-1-63555-413-7)

The House by Eden Darry. After a vicious assault, Sadie, Fin, and their family retreat to a house they think is the perfect place to start over, until they realize not all is as it seems. (978-1-63555-395-6)

Uninvited by Jane C. Esther. When Aerin McLeary's body becomes host for an alien intent on invading Earth, she must work with researcher Olivia Ando to uncover the truth and save humankind. (978-1-63555-282-9)

Comrade Cowgirl by Yolanda Wallace. When cattle rancher Laramie Bowman accepts a lucrative job offer far from home, will her heart end up getting lost in translation? (978-1-63555-375-8)

Double Vision by Ellie Hart. When her cell phone rings, Giselle Cutler answers it—and finds herself speaking to a dead woman. (978-1-63555-385-7)

Inheritors of Chaos by Barbara Ann Wright. As factions splinter and reunite, will anyone survive the final showdown between gods and mortals on an alien world? (978-1-63555-294-2)

Love on Lavender Lane by Karis Walsh. Accompanied by the buzz of honeybees and the scent of lavender, Paige and Kassidy must find a way to compromise on their approach to business if they want to save Lavender Lane Farm—and find a way to make room for love along the way. (978-1-63555-286-7)

Spinning Tales by Brey Willows. When the fairy tale begins to unravel and villains are on the loose, will Maggie and Kody be able to spin a new tale? (978-1-63555-314-7)

The Do-Over by Georgia Beers. Bella Hunt has made a good life for herself and put the past behind her. But when the bane of her high school existence shows up for Bella's class on conflict resolution, the last thing they expect is to fall in love. (978-1-63555-393-2)

What Happens When by Samantha Boyette. For Molly Kennan, senior year is already an epic disaster, and falling for mysterious waitress Zia is about to make life a whole lot worse. (978-1-63555-408-3)

Wooing the Farmer by Jenny Frame. When fiercely independent modern socialite Penelope Huntingdon-Stewart and traditional country farmer Sam McQuade meet, trusting their hearts is harder than it looks. (978-1-63555-381-9)

A Chapter on Love by Laney Webber. When Jannika and Lee reunite, their instant connection feels like a gift, but neither is ready for a second chance at love. Will they finally get on the same page when it comes to love? (978-1-63555-366-6)

Drawing Down the Mist by Sheri Lewis Wohl. Everyone thinks Grand Duchess Maria Romanova died in 1918. They were almost right. (978-1-63555-341-3)

Listen by Kris Bryant. Lily Croft is inexplicably drawn to Hope D'Marco but will she have the courage to confront the consequences of her past and present colliding? (978-1-63555-318-5)

Perfect Partners by Maggie Cummings. Elite police dog trainer Sara Wright has no intention of falling in love with a coworker, until Isabel Marquez arrives at Homeland Security's Northeast Regional Training facility and Sara's good intentions start to falter. (978-1-63555-363-5)

Shut Up and Kiss Me by Julie Cannon. What better way to spend two weeks of hell in paradise than in the company of a hot, sexy woman? (978-1-63555-343-7)

Spencer's Cove by Missouri Vaun. When Foster Owen and Abigail Spencer meet they uncover a story of lives adrift, loves lost, and true love found. (978-1-63555-171-6)

Without Pretense by TJ Thomas. After living for decades hiding from the truth, can Ava learn to trust Bianca with her secrets and her heart? (978-1-63555-173-0)

Unexpected Lightning by Cass Sellars. Lightning strikes once more when Sydney and Parker fight a dangerous stranger who threatens the peace they both desperately want. (978-1-163555-276-8)

Emily's Art and Soul by Joy Argento. When Emily meets Andi Marino she thinks she's found a new best friend but Emily doesn't know that Andi is fast falling in love with her. Caught up in exploring her sexuality, will Emily see the only woman she needs is right in front of her? (978-1-63555-355-0)

Escape to Pleasure: Lesbian Travel Erotica edited by Sandy Lowe and Victoria Villasenor. Join these award-winning authors as they explore the sensual side of erotic lesbian travel. (978-1-63555-339-0)

Music City Dreamers by Robyn Nyx. Music can bring lovers together. In Music City, it can tear them apart. (978-1-63555-207-2)

Ordinary is Perfect by D. Jackson Leigh. Atlanta marketing superstar Autumn Swan's life derails when she inherits a country home, a child, and a very interesting neighbor. (978-1-63555-280-5)

Royal Court by Jenny Frame. When royal dresser Holly Weaver's passionate personality begins to melt Royal Marine Captain Quincy's icy heart, will Holly be ready for what she exposes beneath? (978-1-63555-290-4)

Strings Attached by Holly Stratimore. Success. Riches. Music. Passion. It's a life most can only dream of, but stardom comes at a cost. (978-1-63555-347-5)

The Ashford Place by Jean Copeland. When Isabelle Ashford inherits an old house in small-town Connecticut, family secrets, a shocking discovery, and an unexpected romance complicate her plan for a fast profit and a temporary stay. (978-1-63555-316-1)

Treason by Gun Brooke. Zoem Malderyn's existence is a deadly threat to everyone on Gemocon and Commander Neenja KahSandra must find a way to save the woman she loves from having to commit the ultimate sacrifice. (978-1-63555-244-7)

A Wish Upon a Star by Jeannie Levig. Erica Cooper has learned to depend on only herself, but when her new neighbor, Leslie Raymond, befriends Erica's special needs daughter, the walls protecting her heart threaten to crumble. (978-1-63555-274-4)

Answering the Call by Ali Vali. Detective Sept Savoie returns to the streets of New Orleans, as do the dead bodies from ritualistic killings, and she does everything in her power to bring them to justice while trying to keep her partner, Keegan Blanchard, safe. (978-1-63555-050-4)

Breaking Down Her Walls by Erin Zak. Could a love worth staying for be the key to breaking down Julia Finch's walls? (978-1-63555-369-7)

Exit Plans for Teenage Freaks by 'Nathan Burgoine. Cole always has a plan—especially for escaping his small-town reputation as "that kid who was kidnapped when he was four"—but when he teleports to a museum, it's time to face facts: it's possible he's a total freak after all. (978-1-63555-098-6)

Friends Without Benefits by Dena Blake. When Dex Putman gets the woman she thought she always wanted, she soon wonders if it's really love after all. (978-1-63555-349-9)

Invalid Evidence by Stevie Mikayne. Private Investigator Jil Kidd is called away to investigate a possible killer whale, just when her partner Jess needs her most. (978-1-63555-307-9)

Pursuit of Happiness by Carsen Taite. When attorney Stevie Palmer's client reveals a scandal that could derail Senator Meredith Mitchell's presidential bid, their chance at love may be collateral damage. (978-1-63555-044-3)

Seascape by Karis Walsh. Marine biologist Tess Hansen returns to Washington's isolated northern coast where she struggles to adjust to small-town living while courting an endowment for her orca research center from Brittany James. (978-1-63555-079-5)

Second in Command by VK Powell. Jazz Perry's life is disrupted and her career jeopardized when she becomes personally involved with the case of an abandoned child and the child's competent but strict social worker, Emory Blake. (978-1-63555-185-3)

Taking Chances by Erin McKenzie. When Valerie Cruz and Paige Wellington clash over what's in the best interest of the children in Valerie's care, the children may be the ones who teach them it's worth taking chances for love. (978-1-63555-209-6)